D1625121

GREGORY MONE

AMULET BOOKS • NEW YORK

Cataloging-in-Publication Data has been applied for and may be obtained from the Library of Congress.

ISBN 978-1-4197-5683-2

Text © 2023 Gregory Mone
Jacket, interior, and map illustrations by Berat Pekmezci
Edited by Howard W. Reeves
Book design by Chelsea Hunter

An earlier version of this story was originally published under the title *Fish* in 2010.

Printed and bound in U.S.A.
10 9 8 7 6 5 4 3 2 1

Amulet Books are available at special discounts when purchased in quantity for premiums and promotions as well as fundraising or educational use. Special editions can also be created to specification. For details, contact specialsales@abramsbooks.com or the address below.

Amulet Books® is a registered trademark of Harry N. Abrams, Inc.

ABRAMS The Art of Books
195 Broadway, New York, NY 10007
abramsbooks.com

To the Orient Point Treasure Hunting Society

Contents

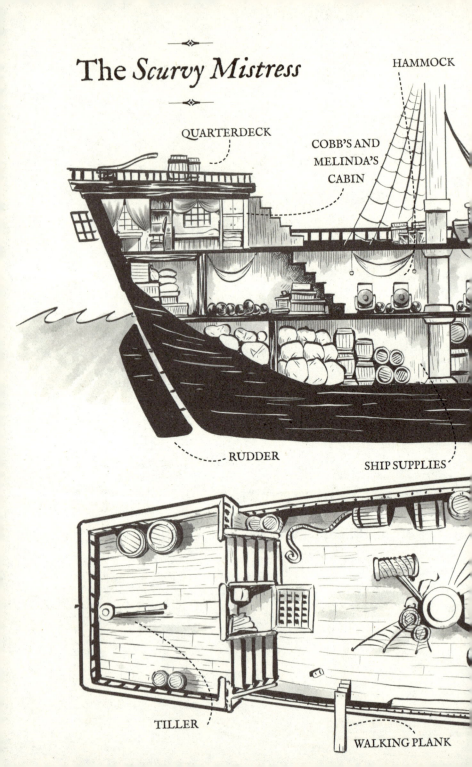

The *Scurvy Mistress*

HAMMOCK

QUARTERDECK

COBB'S AND
MELINDA'S
CABIN

RUDDER

SHIP SUPPLIES

TILLER

WALKING PLANK

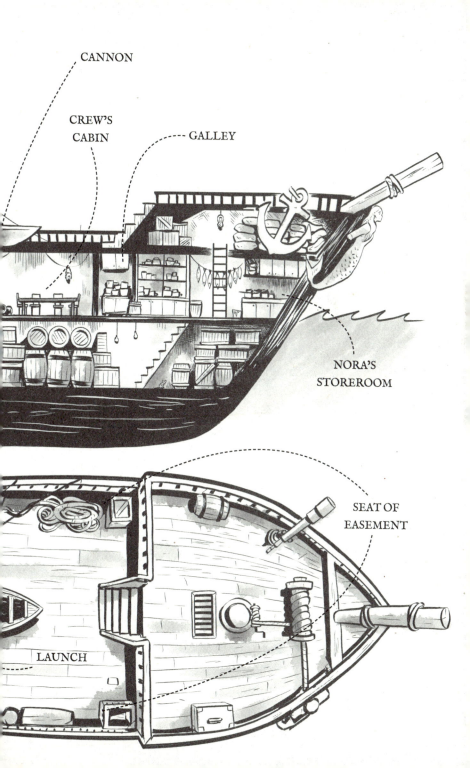

CANNON

CREW'S
CABIN

GALLEY

NORA'S
STOREROOM

SEAT OF
EASEMENT

LAUNCH

1

Fish on a Farm

The rain had been falling heavily for weeks. The rivers could hold no more water; they flooded farms and towns all across Ireland, and the Reidy home was no exception. Several inches of water had gathered on the floor of the cottage on the day Maurice, the fifth child of Fergal and Brigid Reidy, was born. Years later, when Fergal learned that his son had chosen a life at sea, he would think of those floods. He would wonder if the boy felt at home on the open ocean because he'd entered the world surrounded by water.

The floods did stop eventually, and Maurice grew up in a dry and increasingly crowded home. Patrick was the oldest child, followed by Michael, Mary, and Conor, then Maurice, Roisin, Kathleen, Patricia, and, finally, the youngest, Maureen. The Reidys were farmers, and the kids were expected to help Fergal in the fields, but from an early age it became clear that Maurice wasn't much good at the work. His brothers and sisters were twice as fast, and only too happy to remind him of that fact, especially when their father was within range. They enjoyed torturing him in other ways, too, but he had a friend and ally in Roisin. If Michael or Conor snuck a worm into his shoe, she'd be the one to warn him. And whenever Queen Mary, as they called their older sister, gave Roisin one too many orders, Maurice would help her with the extra chore.

As for his nickname, Fish—that can be traced back to a warm autumn morning. The Reidy boys had just finished marching across three farms and through a wood to a clear and cold lake. They called it Outhouse Lake because Michael would always relieve himself along the shore just moments after they'd arrived. Once a week they'd walk there to bathe, always remaining in the shallows since none of them knew how to swim.

As usual, his brothers started fighting the moment they stepped into the water. Michael and Patrick were typically the chief troublemakers, but their battles were waged in good fun. Conor, on the other hand, was short-tempered, quick to transform an innocent scrap into a bruising brawl. On that particular morning, the boys were wading out when Michael pushed Conor from behind. Conor fell, but returned to his feet quickly, only to find Michael and Patrick laughing. Immediately he burst into a rage. He grabbed a stone from the bottom of the lake and prepared to swing at Michael's head. Fish threw himself at Conor, grasping for his arm. Conor, angrier than ever, picked up his younger brother and hurled him out toward the middle of the lake.

Fish didn't fly far, but it proved to be far enough, past an unseen ledge where the shallow water ended and the deep part of the lake began. He tried to plant his feet on the bottom, thinking they'd land in the silt, but they found only water. Immediately he began to sink.

He heard Michael, Patrick, and Conor all shouting. And then, as he slipped below the surface, he stopped hearing anything at all. The water swallowed him. Unexpectedly, he felt comfortable enveloped by the lake. He moved his hands out and down, pushing against the water. Then he reached high above his head, pulled down as hard as he could past his waist, and his body shot upward. The sunlight shone through the water; he pulled again. Finally, just as it felt like his chest was closing in, he broke through the surface.

At this point, the average child would've headed directly back to shore, into the shallows. Maurice? He smiled, laughed, cheered, and stroked right out into the middle of the lake.

From then on, each week when they returned to Outhouse Lake, Maurice would swim and splash and dive for as long as time would allow. His father came with them on occasion and thought it strange the way his son was so comfortable out in the depths. But he had no articulate comment on his behavior; he merely grunted. His mother, when she heard what he was doing, found it downright unacceptable. "I'm trying to raise a man," she said, "not a fish!"

That is how he acquired his name. Of course, the name had little to do with his appearance: he had no gills and no fins. He was a skinny kid, with short, reddish-brown hair, hazel eyes shielded by long lashes, slightly oversize front teeth, and a small nose dotted with faded brown freckles. In his looks, therefore, he was very much a boy, yet his brothers and sisters began calling him Fish, not Maurice, and it felt natural. He was at home in the water.

This discovery turned out to be an important one, given the fact that two years later, thanks to a dead horse, a mildly mysterious uncle, and a young thief, he would find himself on a pirate ship, leaving Ireland behind him for good.

2

The Pirate Thief

Early one fall evening, when Fish was eleven years old, his father slumped into the cottage and announced, "Shamrock is dead."

Shamrock was the family horse and arguably its most valuable member, after Fergal and Brigid. Without Shamrock, the farm would fail. Their few cows and pigs wouldn't produce enough for the family to earn a living. And without Shamrock to plow the fields they'd barely be able to grow enough to feed themselves. "To make ends meet," Fergal declared, "one of you children will have to go work in the city for your uncle Gerry." The money wouldn't be a great amount, but it would help keep the family afloat. Patrick volunteered—he was the oldest—but he was too good of a farmhand to lose. There was really no question of who would have to go, given the fact that he was miserable at farming, often needing half a day to finish a task that any of his siblings could complete in an hour. Fergal decided it would have to be Fish.

His heart raced when his father told him. When his mother placed her hand on his shoulder, he wasn't sure whether to cry or smile. That evening after dinner, she asked him to join her outside as the others cleaned up. The sky was dark and clear. She stared quietly into the distance above the trees at the far end of their field. Any moments alone with one of his parents were extremely rare. And when he stole one with his mother, he'd usually spend most of it listening. She'd talk of her own brothers and sisters, her parents, the farm on which she'd been raised, and how they'd walk, a few times a year, over the hills and down to the sea. These stories would summon a kind of excitement in his mother, an energy she normally kept hidden. Now, although she said little and told no tales, Fish could sense that same energy.

Quietly they stood together, and as the wind rose and swept through the trees, she breathed in deeply through her nose, turned to face him, and planted a gentle kiss on his forehead. After giving his shoulders a squeeze, she nodded once, affirmatively. "You'll do fine," she said, and turned back inside to rejoin the others.

For the next few days, as he prepared to leave, his emotions rose and fell like the ocean waves he'd soon come to love. He'd miss his brothers and sisters, his gruff, hard father and practical mother, his swims in the lake. But the prospect of actually helping his family made him feel a full head taller.

On the day he departed, the good-byes were short and consisted mostly of affectionate punches and brief hugs. Conor's punch wasn't entirely affectionate; he left a painful memento on Fish's shoulder in the form of a purple-and-blue bruise. His mother held him in her arms longer than she ever had before, and his sister Roisin, who could carve just about anything from a hunk of wood, handed him a newly whittled fish. "For my brother the swimmer," she said.

To REACH THE CITY, Fish walked with his father for three solid days along a puddle-filled road traveled by folks on horseback and the occasional carriage. The first night, they slept beneath the stars. The next, they lodged in a large stable, taunted by the sights, sounds, and smells of healthy horses, and they finally arrived in the city late on the third day. Fish had never seen more than three buildings in one place. Here there were hundreds, all crammed together and standing three times as tall as the cottage on the farm. The color had been drained from everything; the familiar green fields and trees were gone, replaced with varying shades of brown. The entire city looked like it needed a bath.

Smoke billowed from chimneys and doorways, burning his nostrils. The heavenly scents of freshly baked breads and roasted meats mingled with the foul stench of over-flowing outhouses and trash-lined alleys. One moment he wanted to savor the air, the next he felt like wrapping a cloth around his mouth and nose.

Fish stayed close to his father as they pushed through the crowded streets. Eventually, Fergal turned into a public house—a dark and miserable wooden cave that blocked out all sunlight. The patrons were all huddled together in small groups with their backs to the door. Only a few of them looked up when Fish and his father entered.

Then a large man with large hands, standing with his back to the bar, stepped forward. "That's your uncle Gerry," Fergal muttered as the man steered them into a tight booth. There were no hugs or handshakes between the brothers. Uncle Gerry insisted on taking the seat facing the door, then ordered two ales for himself and his brother.

His father and Uncle Gerry grunted and grumbled back and forth. Although it sounded like they both had food stuck in their throats, Fish knew that they were, in their own way, conducting a very real conversation.

Finally, Fish heard his father say, "So it's decided, then."

He turned to his father. What was decided?

"Frgggghhhh," Uncle Gerry responded.

"Gruffff," his father answered.

Fergal stepped out of the booth. Fish slid toward the end, ready to follow his dad, but Uncle Gerry reached across the table and placed one of his large hands on Fish's shoulder, stopping him. The hand was heavy, cold, and hard. Fish looked up at his father. "Where are you going?"

"Home," his father answered. "You'll stay here now." Fergal picked up his glass, drank the last of the brown ale, then set it down with finality. He placed his hand on Fish's head. "Be careful, son," he said, "and good luck."

At the time, Fish had no idea these were the last words he'd ever hear from his father.

THE FIRST FEW WEEKS in the city passed slowly. Fish desperately missed his brothers and sisters, those rare moments around the table when nobody was fighting and everyone was full of food and cheer. But soon the city pulled his mind away from thoughts of home. Winding streets and narrow alleyways fed off wide thoroughfares lined with people selling vegetables, wool, and various trinkets out of wooden carts. Sailors and merchants spoke Portuguese, French, Italian, and, of course, Irish.

Fish didn't exactly understand what sort of business Uncle Gerry conducted. They lived and worked in a small, two-room office on the second floor of a narrow brick building. Fish slept on a mattress in a corner of the front room, between his uncle's desk and a tall window. Each morning he'd roll up his bed and tuck it away, out of sight of any potential clients. None of his clothes fit him; they were all oversize hand-me-downs from his older brothers.

His too-large shirts were especially annoying, but he'd tuck them in and do his best to look presentable. Then he'd spend his day carrying packages of various shapes and sizes from one part of the city to another and recording every job and errand he completed in a leather-bound notebook. Fish ran letters to the crowded and frightful prison, delivered items to the breweries, whisked notes from the grand houses on the city's edges to boats down at the docks. These last jobs were his favorites, since they brought him near the water. He loved to race down, close his eyes, and breathe in the sea air. He'd get close to the boats, inspect their hulls, decks, and sails for signs of distant adventures. He could almost smell the open ocean on their sails. Yet he never lingered too long. His uncle had enough clients to keep him moving from morning until night, when Fish would collapse, exhausted, onto his small bed.

Despite his fatigue, Fish never complained. He worked ever harder and faster, straight through the rest of fall, winter, and spring. He asked Uncle Gerry when he might have a break so he could visit home, but his uncle only grunted. Fish sent his earnings to his family on a regular basis, but he rarely heard back, and the few replies he did receive were short. He wondered if anyone at home actually missed him. Sometimes he rubbed the fish Roisin gave him, as if this might magically bring him back to the farm.

One summer afternoon, as he returned from an errand,

Uncle Gerry held out a leather purse. "You will bring this to the docks . . . why are you smiling?"

Fish tried to straighten out his mouth. "Sorry, sir. I like being near the water."

"This is an important task."

"Of course, sir."

His uncle's eyes narrowed. Fish had stopped smiling, right? Yes, he was certain of it. His face was as blank as a paving stone.

"You will deliver this package," his uncle continued, "to a man named Reginald Swift. He is an uncommonly small man with uncommonly large eyeglasses, and he is expecting you."

Fish extended his open hand. Uncle Gerry grunted, glowered, grunted again, then leaned forward and dropped the heavy purse into his palm. The sound, the feel—Fish was certain it was filled with coins. "Are these—"

"The contents are not your concern."

Fish turned to leave, but his uncle stopped him. "Fish?"

"Yes, sir?" he asked.

"I realize that I stress the importance of all your assignments, but this one is especially critical. These particular clients . . . they do not tolerate mistakes. You must not fail."

Fish replied with a solemn nod, then tucked his notebook into his waistband and sped out the door, down the street, and through the alleys he'd come to know so well.

Within minutes he'd reached the harbor. A grand, beautiful ship he'd never seen before, the *Mary*, was tied up in one of the slips. Sailors were rolling huge wooden barrels filled with water, beer, salted pork and beef, biscuits, and butter up onto her deck.

The docks and their surroundings were unusually crowded. What had Uncle Gerry said about the man? Uncommonly small, with uncommonly large eyeglasses. Fish wondered just how small someone had to be to qualify as uncommonly so. He stopped as a short, bald man stepped toward him. No, that wouldn't be Reginald Swift. He didn't have glasses.

Another possible candidate leaned against the wall outside a pub with his face turned to the sun. A woman burst through the door, grabbed him by the arm, and ordered him to get back to work. Standing upright, he wasn't quite as small as Fish had thought. Then the man's boss noticed Fish. "What are you looking at, you lazy cur?" she growled.

Fish turned away and hurried on. All around him, vendors were calling out prices. Boys his age were announcing the latest news from the high seas, selling pamphlets and the one-sheet newspapers known as broadsides. A young woman with a thin scar on her face and a sword at her side sneered in his direction. Fish pushed forward. A quartet of ladies in very large yellow dresses briefly blocked his way. He squeezed between them, then spotted a man leaning against one of the piers' tall, worn wooden columns. A fine ship was tied to the dock behind him. Not as large as the *Mary*, but just as beautiful—a boat that appeared equally suited for crossing the ocean or hosting a cocktail party for the city's wealthiest citizens. Fish turned his attention back to the man. Short? Very much so. When a sailor walked in front of the fellow, he looked like a child. The glasses, too, matched Uncle Gerry's description. Big and black-rimmed, they took up nearly half his face. This had to be Swift. And his glasses were effective, for his eyes widened greedily as he spotted the purse.

Fish pressed back his shoulders and stood taller. A wave of pride washed through him. Uncle Gerry had entrusted him with a very important task, and he was about to complete it successfully. Would Uncle Gerry tell his father? Fish imagined his dad clapping him proudly on the back, the way he'd congratulate Patrick, Michael, and Conor after a hard day's work in the—

Someone crashed into Fish from behind, driving his shoulder down against the dock. He blinked, breathed, felt a tug on the purse gripped tight in his fingers. His head was spinning. He tried to sit up, but he was yanked up to his feet by his collar. A boy his age grabbed him by his oversize shirt and pulled him close. His breath was uniquely rancid. "Release the purse and I'll release you," the boy snarled.

The boy was strong—even tougher than his brothers—

but Fish wasn't about to fail Uncle Gerry. He closed both hands around the purse and tried to pull away. The boy struck him in the jaw. Stinging pain shot through Fish's head. His ears rang. Was that really necessary? Holding tight to the purse, wrestling with his attacker, Fish muttered, "Can't we . . . discuss this . . . in a more civilized way?"

The boy drove his fist into Fish's stomach.

He crumpled to the dock.

Apparently, the answer was no.

Fish rolled to his side—he felt the journal secured in his waistband, but the purse was gone. A few of the coins had scattered onto the dock in the fight. Fish grabbed them, steadied himself, and stood. His ears were still ringing.

The thief was already hurrying away through the crowd.

Ignoring the pain, Fish ran and leaped at the boy's legs. They grappled toward the edge of the dock, and then his attacker smiled and pushed Fish over the side, sending him splashing down into the cool water below. Immediately, Fish pulled back to the surface, his right fist still clenched around the recovered coins. Treading water, he scoured the docks. The boy was gone. No one seemed to care that Fish had been attacked, either; all the passengers, sailors, and dockworkers were carrying on as before.

A thick rope splashed into the water. The man he believed to be Reginald Swift was up on the dock, urging him to hurry; Fish pulled himself out of the water. A woman old enough to be Fish's grandmother, and a head taller than Swift, stood beside the bespectacled man. Her white, curly hair was pulled up in a bun. Her face was so pale and wrinkled that she could have passed for a ghost, but her blue, bright eyes sparked with life.

"The boy and a man . . . they went that way!" Swift cried, pointing down the dock, "and if you don't catch them, my mother will be furious!"

"Your mother?" Fish asked.

The woman with the bright blue eyes sneered. "I am Lady Swift," she said, "and this is Reginald, my unfortunate excuse for a son. I sincerely hope you do not prove to be an unfortunate excuse for an errand boy."

Fish scrunched his nose. "I'm sorry, I—"

"Sorry? I do not tolerate apologies. Or failure."

Fish unclenched his fist and showed her the coins. "I did recover a few—"

"Useless!" she declared.

"We need all the pieces of the puzzle," Reginald explained, "including the purse. Hurry!"

Lady Swift pointed into the crowd. "Go!"

Dripping wet, his stomach aching from the punch, Fish sprinted into the mass of people. Yet the ruffian boy and his accomplice had disappeared. His heart was pounding. Never mind the threats from Lady Swift and her son. What would Uncle Gerry say? He couldn't disappoint his uncle, his father and mother. He had to find the thieves.

The crowd thinned, and he spotted the pair in a row-boat, moving quickly toward the other side of the harbor. There, anchored near the shore, floated a thoroughly menacing ship.

3

Stealing from Scalawags

ish stripped off his shirt and tied it around his waist, then kicked off his shoes—which were, incidentally, the last pair of shoes he'd own—and leaped headfirst into the cool harbor. The rowboat was too far ahead and moving too quickly. There was no way he could catch it, so he swam slowly and quietly with his head barely above the water, hoping the thieves wouldn't hear or see him. If he could somehow climb up onto the ship and find the purse, then he could slip back down into the water and swim for shore without anyone noticing. That was sure to work, he decided.

Fish had learned a fact or two about ships since he'd been working in the city. This craft, from the size and shape of it, and the way its single mast leaned toward the back, was a sloop. One of the dockworkers had told him they were fast, easy to handle, capable of holding fifty men or more. The man had also said they were favored by a certain class of seafaring men known as pirates, but Fish pushed this frightening notion to the back of his mind. Not every sloop was crewed by pirates! The boy and his partner were probably just common thieves. They were not pirates. Of course not.

He swam toward the front of the ship, where a long, thick, slimy cable ran down from the boat to an anchor on the harbor floor. Normally, oceangoing craft had a wooden statue of some sort at the bow, a beautiful maiden or mermaid. But this ship's figurehead resembled a monster: charred, cut, and slashed in places, all of its paint chipped or worn. One of the arms looked like it had been sawed off at the elbow, too. The point of these statues was to win the ocean's favor by presenting her with a beautiful figure. In that effort, this boat offered nothing but insult.

Luckily, though, no one stood watch above that monstrous mermaid. If Fish moved fast, he could reach the deck undetected. He scurried up the slimy cable, grabbed the wooden railing at the bow, jumped over, and crouched low. As he pulled on his shirt, he felt the notebook at his waist and silently scolded himself; he should've stashed it somewhere before diving into the water.

The men on deck were clearly not regular merchants or sailors. They did not wear uniforms; their clothes were mostly ragged and worn, patched together in several places, as if each shirt had been sewn together from the remains of five or six others. Every size, shape, and color of man seemed crowded onto the deck, and these rough and wind-whipped rogues wore leather belts and braces packed with pistols and blades.

There was no denying it now.

The men were pirates.

Naturally, Fish had heard about pirates. Stories of these seagoing adventurers had reached the farm on occasion, and they were often talked about in the city, where people departing for the long sail to America hoped and prayed aloud that they wouldn't be raided along the way.

Now he was attempting to rob a group of these rogues.

Or steal back what belonged to someone else, at least.

A large section of a folded-up sail was lying flat on the deck beside him. Fish grabbed the thick canvas, hoping to dry his face and hands.

"Go on with you!" a man yelled without looking up. "I'm working!"

The man was hunched over the far end of the sailcloth, busy with needle and thread. He was entirely bald, with a bright red face, small eyes, and hollow cheeks that suggested he didn't eat well. His clothes were nothing like those of his shipmates—the cuffs and collar of his shirt looked to be made from the finest fabrics, with gilded buttons that shone in the sunlight.

Fish hurried away. The other men were similarly preoccupied. A few were scrubbing the deck, others were stowing heavy oaken barrels down below, still more were sharpening long, gleaming blades on rough gray stones. All of them were toiling at their tasks except for a small group standing before the lone cabin, at the far end of the boat.

The thief was with them, his chest puffed out. His pose reminded Fish of the way Patrick would stand when he was talking to their parents, trying to act older. Patrick would press his shoulders back, keep his chin high, and scrunch his forehead as if it were a gargantuan task to keep all the large and important thoughts in his head from rushing out at once. This boy, too, was trying to appear wise beyond his years.

A large, worn brush with a long handle leaned against a nearby railing; Fish grabbed it and walked with his head down, idly sweeping the floor.

Stopping short of the group, Fish crouched beside a railing that ran along the side of the ship. Four other pirates stood with the young thief, including a woman with bright orange hair. Fish could now see the boy had lightly freckled skin, much like Michael, though it was also tinted brown from the sun. His hair was straight, short, and dark brown, and his arms were more muscular than those of Fish's brothers.

One of the men—the leader, Fish guessed—looked to be about his father's age. He had tightly curled gray hair and fine clothes, and held the stem of an unlit pipe between his lips. A thin, pronounced nose added to his general air of nobility. His ears were large, pressed back flat against his head; his skin was tanned, and a faded but thick red scar slashed across his chin.

The man on his right, who had been with the thief in the boat, was the shortest among them, and more vile than noble. He had long black hair, a ragged beard, and dark eyes hiding beneath bushy, unkempt eyebrows. Dull silver hoops were stuck through his lower lip and ears. He was tremendously thick, as if he'd been hit on the head with a massive hammer and compacted into that short frame, and old scars slashed across his forehead, both cheeks, and his chin.

The final pirate was an absolute giant. He was a human oak tree. His large nose, bent in the middle, leaned to one side near the tip. His dark, thick beard looked rough enough to sand the wooden deck smooth, and he scratched it with fingers as large as sausages.

The giant, the woman, and the boy were quiet; the other two were arguing.

The short, thick man grabbed the purse. "Treachery! That's what I call this, Cobb."

"Captain Cobb," the other man stressed.

"You won't be captain for long if you betray your crew. Not even your giant friend here could calm fifty angry, armed men."

The captain traced the scar on his chin. His voice

turned quiet and serious. "I have not betrayed my crew, Scab. You disobeyed me; you were not supposed to accompany Nate."

"Why do you think I joined him? I might not have been educated at Cambridge, but I am no fool," the other pirate growled. He held out the purse. "Do you mean to tell me that you sent this boy ashore simply to steal a bag of coins? Can you honestly say that this has nothing to do with your beloved chain?"

"Scab," the woman cut in, her voice calm, "I don't think—"

"Don't defend him, Melinda," the pirate called Scab growled back. "Tell me, Cobb, can you assure the men that you do not plan to enlist us in yet another fruitless quest for that mythical string of jewels? Nate," he said, turning to the boy, "would you rather cross the ocean in search of something that might not exist? Or would you follow the course of a right-minded pirate and patrol the shipping and transit lanes for frigates and galleons loaded with goods and riches?"

Fish watched the boy, Nate, hesitate. "I . . ."

"Nathaniel," Cobb said, "you don't have to answer that. Now give me my purse, Scab."

"It doesn't belong to you."

All five of the pirates turned toward Fish.

Had he actually said that aloud? He stared down at the

deck and dropped to one knee. Perhaps they'd ignore him if he resumed scrubbing. The sharp edge of a blade, held under his chin, informed him otherwise.

"Up," Scab growled.

"That's the courier," said Nate. "The one who was carrying the purse."

"And you're here to retrieve your package?" Cobb asked.

Fish couldn't think with that piece of metal against his skin. The pirate grabbed the soaked notebook from his waistband and tossed it aside onto the deck.

"Scab," Cobb said, "lower your blade."

The pirate stepped away. Fish exhaled and tried to stand taller. He felt so thin and weak in his soaked shirt; he coughed and deepened his voice. "Yes. I am here to retrieve it."

"This was stolen from you?" Scab asked. "How terrible! An absolute scandal in a perfectly reputable city such as this. Here, take it back. It's yours."

The pirate dropped the purse into Fish's open palm. He felt the weight of the coins in his hand. Was that all? Yes, apparently so. And here Fish had been thinking that pirates were irrational, greedy rogues! Yet there was some honor among them. He thanked the surprisingly noble scalawag and took a half step toward his notebook.

Unfortunately, it wasn't going to be that easy.

Nate lunged at him, grabbing at the purse.

Scab stepped between them.

Fish looked down at the purse in his hand. The railing—he glanced to his right—was only a few steps away.

He might reach the shore before they caught him in that rowboat. The captain was watching Fish, squinting with intense curiosity. His idea was probably a terrible one, but he did have the purse. Fish sprang up onto the railing and dove off the side of the ship.

4

Reluctant Recruit

The shore wasn't far, but he needed both hands to swim quickly, so he ducked under the water, took one end of the rope he used as a belt, tied it around the purse, then resurfaced. He'd only taken a few strokes when he heard the loud splash in the water behind him. The men were all at the railing, yelling and pointing. Somebody was in the water, but if he was trying to chase Fish, he was failing miserably. The man wasn't swimming. He was drowning.

Fish guessed it was Nate, the boy who had stolen the purse in the first place. But no—the man in the water was bearded, his face home to numerous silver hoops. The pirate called Scab was flailing and waving his arms.

A moment later, he went under. Bubbles popped at the surface. Fish waited, watching. He eyed the rogues at the railing. No one was diving in to save the man. Fish glanced in the other direction. The shore opposite the docks was even closer than he'd realized. But if he swam away, then Scab might die.

And Fish could not let that happen.

He kicked back toward the boat, breathed in deep, and dove. The water was dark and slightly murky, but he followed the shower of bubbles and found the drowning man quickly; Scab had sunk like a rock. Fish grabbed him by the shirt, pulled with his one free hand, and kicked with all his might toward the surface.

When they emerged, the pirate was limp and lifeless. A few of the men on deck cheered as Fish swam him to the anchor cable. The red-haired woman, Melinda, was watching from the railing. A girl and a brown-skinned boy stood at her side. Fish grabbed hold of the cable, then pulled Scab's hands toward it, too. The feel of something solid brought the pirate back to life. Relieved, Fish smiled. Surely they'd help him now. He'd saved one of their men! They'd be obliged to let him return to shore with Mr. Swift's purse. Maybe they'd even give him a reward. A few coins, perhaps? Or some kind of jewel? He'd be thrilled if he could send a necklace or ring back to his mother. She'd probably trade it for a donkey, but the gift would still mean something.

Unfortunately, his reward was a cold metal blade to his neck. The smell of the pirate's sharp, stinking breath filled his nostrils, carrying undercurrents of old onions and hints of something even more potent. Was it unwashed feet? Scab flashed a crooked, false, spine-shivering smile. His teeth were brown and broken, his breath hot. His voice sounded like it was coming from deep inside a dungeon. "You should have let me sink," he growled.

Scab pulled away his weapon. He bit down on the blade with his cracked teeth and climbed up the cable with surprising speed.

Fish looked to the shore. He could still escape underwater.

Above him, he heard a distinctive click.

Then another.

And a third.

On deck, three pirates were aiming their pistols at him. The captain pointed at Fish. "Up," he said. "Now."

When Fish climbed over the railing, Scab was bellowing at the captain, roaring with anger. "The men deserve a prize, Cobb, not a dream!" he yelled. "They deserve a prize!"

The giant, who hadn't said a word since Fish had been on board, wrapped his massive fingers around the boy's shoulders. Fish suspected those fingers could have cracked his bones as easily as eggshells, so he did not resist when the mountainous pirate pushed him toward the rear of the ship, where the captain waited. He dared not refuse when the man held out his hand for the purse, either. Fish glanced at the girl. She eyed him coldly.

Meanwhile, Scab continued his curse-filled rant as two men dragged him away.

Cobb turned to Fish. "You've incited some trouble, friend."

His voice slightly shaky, Fish asked, "Why is he so angry?"

Melinda shook her head. "Because the captain here had Moravius throw him overboard."

"Scab gave the boy the purse! And so it was his responsibility to retrieve it."

"But he doesn't know how to swim," Fish noted.

"That is not my concern," Cobb shot back. "Furthermore, we have a theoretical disagreement with Scab regarding the proper way to operate as a paperless privateer—"

"You mean 'pirate,' right?" Fish asked.

"No," Cobb replied, "I do not—" The captain paused as Melinda elbowed him.

"Before you begin lecturing," she said, "perhaps we should introduce ourselves?" She nodded to Fish. "Melinda Cobb. Cartographer."

The captain placed his hand against his ruffled shirt. "Captain Walter Cobb. My wife, Melinda, and I command this crew, and you ask a more complex question than you realize. A paperless privateer works in the service of one of the great nations, which charges us with attacking the ships of rival countries. As such, we are mostly legitimate soldiers of the sea."

"Mostly?" Fish pressed.

"Mostly," Melinda confirmed.

"Our lack of papers, or official orders, allows our superiors to strike and steal from their enemies while denying any involvement," the captain explained. "In secret they applaud us and in public they call us rogues. Yet that same lack of official documentation allows us to adjust our missions to fit the circumstances. So, when we are within range of the home ports of the Royal Navy, we are paperless privateers. We sail our ship and swing our swords in service of the king and queen. But out on the ocean, we enjoy the freedom to act as we see fit. Out there, or in the calm and welcoming harbors of our next destination, Risden's Isle," he continued, pointing in the direction of the open sea, "we are pirates."

The thin, red-faced pirate Fish had first encountered when he snuck onto the ship suddenly leaned into their conversation. "We're going to Risden's Isle?" he asked.

The giant growled in response.

"Keep that to yourself, will you, Thimble?" Melinda replied.

"And afford us some privacy, man!" Cobb added.

The pirate stepped quickly away.

Fish stared out at the water. Beyond the harbor stretched the open sea. He felt the cool breeze against his face and briefly closed his eyes. The sea air tasted of salt. He relaxed slightly. The air, the water, the people—this was far more civilized than all the screaming and fighting. He'd finally met a few reasonable people. "So, this theoretical disagreement—"

"No more questions!" Cobb snapped. "Right now the only question is what we are going to do with you." The captain looked to Melinda, who shrugged.

"Another deckhand wouldn't hurt," she said.

All around him, the crew was busily working. The pirates were pulling up anchor, hoisting sails, shouting orders from one side of the ship to the other. The sloop, Fish realized, was leaving the harbor.

The purse was in Cobb's hands now. And it was clearly a source of controversy. Fish had a simple solution. "Or you can return my property and let me go."

"Your property?" Cobb laughed. He tossed the purse to Melinda.

She inspected the contents briefly, then passed them to the giant. "There is no rightful owner to the contents of this purse," she said. "It belongs to whoever is intelligent or resourceful enough to have it in their possession."

"Thus, at present, it is very much ours," the captain continued, and nodded to the giant, Moravius. "Take that into my cabin."

The giant walked off without a word; Melinda soon rushed to his side.

"I do admire your perseverance, young man," Cobb added. "You handle yourself well in the water. As you saw, none of the men dove in to save Scab. They could not save him because they cannot swim. This skill is all too rare, I'm afraid." Delicately scratching his curls, he squinted. "What's your name?"

Fish started to say "Maurice," then corrected himself. "Fish."

"Yes, of course! How fitting." The captain's eyebrows angled down as he studied Fish intensely. The look of deep concentration reminded Fish of the way his father would inspect a sheep or pig on sale at the market. "A proficiency in swimming. An unyielding commitment to assigned tasks. Some intriguing qualities for a pirate." He grabbed Fish's hands and turned them over. "Small. They don't look like they have seen a day of hard work."

Fish yanked his hands away. What an insult! And a completely inaccurate one. No, he didn't spend his days yanking on ropes aboard a sailing ship, but he worked as hard as anyone. This man, who had known him for all of a few minutes, had no right to say otherwise. "I resent—"

Cobb cut him off. "We do need another boy aboard. Someone to swab the decks, clean the seats of easement, assist the gunners . . . Given your talent for swimming, I suppose you could scrape the hull when we are at anchor. There's no time now, but perhaps at Risden's Isle. A barnacle-free boat makes for far smoother sailing, you know." The captain took his pipe and jabbed the mouthpiece into the air. "Still, I can't just *give* you a position on the crew. The men don't take the dispensation of shares lightly. Every time we add a sailor, even a lowly deckhand, the men get a slightly smaller piece of any future loot. You'll have to prove your worth to join us. So, we'll consider this a trial."

Fish had no intention of becoming a pirate. He would've rejected the idea immediately. But there was a chance he could still escape with the purse and complete his assignment. The shore wasn't too far. He could steal it back and flee. For now, though, he had to play along. "And if I don't prove useful?"

The captain patted him firmly on the shoulder and smiled. "Then we toss you overboard," he said, "and you swim your way home."

One of the sails snapped full with wind, and the ship began edging forward.

Several of the buccaneers cheered.

Fish noticed the red-faced pirate, Thimble, stuff a rolled-up piece of paper into an otherwise empty bottle, insert a stopper, and drop it into the sea. As the skinny rogue glanced furtively from side to side, Fish turned his gaze elsewhere. Clearly, Thimble was trying to be discreet, and the last thing Fish needed to do was anger another one of the crew.

The captain called over the brown-skinned boy whom Fish had seen at the railing. "Daniel, meet your new assistant. Would you kindly show him how to freshen up this wood?"

Daniel agreed, and Cobb returned to his cabin. The boy had very short black hair, tightly curled, and brown eyes with hints of green. He was about Fish's age and height, but his shoulders were broad, and he had the rough, weathered hands of someone much older. His pants had several large pockets, one of which was stuffed with papers. Daniel handed Fish the brush with the long wooden handle he'd used earlier. "Welcome to the *Scurvy Mistress*," he said. "This is a swab, and you will soon think of it as a third arm."

"Excuse me?" he said. "The what?"

"The *Scurvy Mistress*. That's her name."

"Her?"

"The ship!"

"Oh, right."

"You've never sailed before?"

"No, I . . ."

Throwing his arm around Fish's shoulders, Daniel pointed to the front of the ship, then the back, right, and left. In turn, he said, "Bow. Stern. Starboard. Larboard. Got that?" Fish nodded. "Good. Remember that, stay out of everyone's way, and you might survive. *Might*." Daniel pointed at the swab. "You have to work, though, if you're going to be part of this crew."

"I'm not a part of the crew yet."

Daniel shrugged. "Well, I'd advise you to do what I do or else one of these ugly gentlemen will slam the butt of a pistol into your head. Which is, I assure you, not a particularly enjoyable experience." He pointed to his right ear. "I don't hear much out of this side, thanks to one such strike."

Fish needed no further convincing. He mimicked Daniel, pressed the swab to the slimy wooden surface, and began scrubbing. Then Daniel stopped, reached behind his back, and removed a small, sodden notebook. "Almost forgot," he said. "This is yours." Before handing it back, Daniel thumbed through the mostly blank pages. "You've barely written in it! What a waste of fine paper."

"It's ruined now."

"A day or two in the sun and these pages will be dried out and good as new," Daniel replied.

Fish eyed the papers in Daniel's pockets. Obviously, he was a reader. The boy was unusually interested in the notebook. And Uncle Gerry had dozens of them. "Keep it," Fish said. "It's yours if you want it."

After a brief pause, Daniel smiled, thanked him, and tucked the notebook away again. "I'll dry it out later. Now," Daniel continued, "what do you mean about not being part of this crew?"

"The captain said this is a trial. I'm only here because that thief Nate—"

Daniel laughed. "Nate the Great."

"What?"

"I call him that because he thinks he is going to be some sort of great pirate captain one day."

"Right, well, he stole this purse, so I followed him here to get it back, because if I fail, Uncle Gerry will never let me work for him again, and then I won't be able to send any money back home and my family . . . my family will . . ."

Fish thought of the carving Roisin had given him; did he still have it? He shoved his hands into his pockets. Thankfully, the wooden fish was there. The extra coins, too. He gripped the fish tightly, as if it might give him strength.

"Money? You're concerned about money?" Daniel asked.

No—or maybe, yes? Fish hadn't thought about it this way before, but money was at the root of it all. If money were of no concern, the death of Shamrock wouldn't have been so dire, and he never would have been sent to the city in the first place. "Yes," he said finally. "I suppose I'm concerned about money."

Daniel resumed scrubbing, motioned for Fish to do the same. "If you want money, this is the place to work. What is it that you do now?"

"I'm a messenger."

"Ha! Earning little more than a mat and a meal, I'd guess. Not even enough for a shirt that fits, I see."

Fish tucked in his soaked shirt. "It belonged to one of my brothers. And I suppose you're right. I don't earn much."

"That's fine for most people our age, but not me. I've been on ships my entire life. And I've been privateering, or," he added in a whisper, "pirating, since I was seven."

"You were a pirate at age seven?"

"I'm precocious," Daniel continued. He tapped a few of the papers in his pockets. "I know as much or more about the world of privateering than anyone, and this crew is the best I've sailed with. Captain Cobb is probably the smartest man on the sea, and Scab is one of the toughest, with a feel for the winds and the waves like no one I have ever seen. Noah, our carpenter, has no equal. Then there's Thimble." He pointed toward the red-faced, skeletal man who'd asked where they were going. "He doesn't really love anything but his clothes and his wine. The man can patch anything with a bit of thread, though. Sails, jackets, pants, pirates."

"Pirates?" Fish asked.

"Sure. He's also our surgeon. Sews you up if you've been shot or stabbed," Daniel explained. "Melinda, our navigator, can find her way anywhere with a few glances at the sun and stars. A brilliant mapmaker, too, and she looks out for us kids."

"Right," Fish said, "I saw a girl—"

"Nora!" Daniel replied. "She's a good friend to have, in part because you don't want to be her enemy. She can be as fierce as Scab." Now Daniel pointed to a sailor with a head the size and shape of a melon. "Sammy the Stomach has the appetite of ten men, but more importantly, he's an amazing gunner. He could knock a spyglass out of an opposing captain's hands with a cannonball. That said, most of the time we don't even need to fire a shot. Once the other crews get a glimpse of our resident giant, Moravius, they run the white flag. He could stop a tidal wave with a scowl. Now, you put all these scalawags on a single ship, and you know what that adds up to?"

A group that would give the devil nightmares, Fish thought.

"Gold! I already have more money than my parents ever dreamed of. In four or five years, I should have enough to buy myself and my parents a big house. A house full of friends and food and books. I'll have a library that would make a scholar jealous. Yes," he continued, "if it's money you need, you have to be out on the water. The seas are filled with gold."

Suddenly, Daniel stopped scrubbing and looked toward the back of the ship—the stern, that's what he'd said. All the pirates were putting aside their tools and tasks, walking toward the two boys. Fish spotted Nora climbing up from belowdecks. Daniel motioned for Fish to follow him; they moved to the railing. A black flag was making its way up the mast. Daniel elbowed him. "That means it's time for action," he whispered.

The flag flapped open in the wind, revealing the image of a white hourglass.

"I know, where's the old skull and crossbones, right?" Daniel asked. "Captain Cobb prefers the hourglass. He says it reminds us that our time is limited and that we've got to make the most of it while we can."

In front of his cabin, Cobb coughed twice, then faced the gathered men. Melinda and Moravius stood nearby. Scab, black eyes narrowed beneath his dense eyebrows, was with the gathered rogues. Fish noticed Thimble whispering to him.

The giant pounded his foot against the deck. The pirates fell quiet.

"Our first mate has convinced me that the time has come for us to take a prize," Cobb announced.

Many in the crowd cheered and stomped their feet. Fish could feel the deck shake. Cobb and Scab glared at each other, as if this were just a new, more subtle phase of their argument. Only the smallest hint of a smile—an ugly, unnatural one—appeared on Scab's scarred face.

"At noon tomorrow we will take the *Mary*, a freighter bound for America. Her passengers carry with them tremendous riches, and we plan to relieve the ship of this extra weight, allowing her a smoother, swifter sail across the sea." Another cheer followed. "Begin the preparations!" Cobb ordered.

The crew immediately refocused their efforts.

"What does he mean when he says you're going to 'take' her?" Fish asked Daniel.

The boy was solemn when he answered. "He means we're not pretending to be legitimate agents of the government any longer. We're pirates, Fish, and we're going into battle."

5

No Grime Too Green

Fish spent the remainder of the day brushing the deck free of grime and slime. On several occasions he became so focused on his appointed task that he forgot entirely he was on a pirate ship, working alongside some of the most dangerous men on the high seas. After removing one particularly stubborn stain, he actually smiled with pride. There was a call for supper near the end of the day, but not even the powerful hunger roaring in his stomach convinced him to venture down into the crowded, nightmarish depths of the ship. Thanking Fish again for the notebook, which he said was already drying nicely, Daniel brought him a mug of water and a few rolls. The bread was hard as rock, but he swallowed it down, tucked himself under some sailcloth, and let the boat rock him into a deep sleep.

At dawn, Fish arose to the familiar sound of a cock crowing. He covered his face instinctively; he'd been attacked by his family's rooster so many times that he now had an irrational fear of chickens. Yet this call could not be traced to any shipbound bird. Moravius was standing with his hands cupped to his mouth, crowing. Fish rubbed his eyes with his fists. Was this some kind of dream?

"An odd way to wake us all," Daniel said from behind him, "but it does work."

"He crows?" Fish said.

"Don't ask him why. He won't answer. Doesn't say a word, but he crows each morning like the world's largest rooster. So, how did you sleep?" Fish yawned. "Not enough, I see. I woke up early myself, thought I'd come up here to see if anyone had thrown you overboard during the night."

The handle of a swab smacked Fish in the chest. The stink of rotting onions and feet replaced the delightfully fresh air. Although he'd met him only the day before, Fish could already recognize Scab by scent alone. The pirate spat something black and thick onto the deck, then pointed to the vile glob.

"You were supposed to have this scrubbed yesterday," Scab barked. "Get back to work, you lazy cur!"

Daniel flashed him a look of sympathy, but Fish followed Scab's orders without a word of protest. And he planned to continue behaving for the remainder of the morning. He'd live according to their strange rules until the raid of the *Mary* began.

Then he'd follow his own directives.

Fish was going to launch a raid of his own.

THE *SCURVY MISTRESS* HEADED southwest along the coast, carried along by a steady breeze, passing a stretch of the country his mother once said was more beautiful than heaven itself. She'd been born in these lands, Fish recalled, and probably still had cousins in the area. Bright green hills sat atop ragged, sandy cliffs. The blue-green ocean stretched out before them under a canopy of clear blue sky. On the beach in the distance, he could see farmers collecting seaweed to fertilize their fields.

The pirates were busy preparing for battle. Anything that wasn't part of the deck, or bolted to it, was sent down below. Large pieces of cloth and canvas were hung over the railings. A group of rogues sat near the bow, polishing, inspecting, and loading pistols and muskets. Another sharpened cutlasses and knives.

The call for breakfast came and went. Daniel, who said that he didn't eat a morning meal himself, saved Fish from starving once more, bringing him another few rock-hard rolls, a cold, salty, tough piece of meat, and a mug of grayish, strange-tasting milk. How Daniel went without breakfast he couldn't understand. The food was atrocious, but it was fuel.

With a smile, Daniel produced the notebook. "See? Good as new already. I ran out of writing paper weeks ago, so I really do appreciate the gift."

"What are you writing?" Fish asked.

Daniel shrugged. "Notes, thoughts, observations. I'm sure I'll have plenty to record after today. Now let's get back to work before Scab eyes us chatting."

Late that morning, the *Scurvy Mistress* rounded a point and lingered in a deep, sheltered cove. The water was still, the breeze blocked by the coastal hills. The air was thick with mist and fog, the sun a faded white smear high in the sky. The plan, Fish overheard, was to wait until the *Mary* came within view—they had purposely not advanced too far during the night—and then attack. The *Scurvy Mistress* would have no difficulty overtaking the heavy frigate. She was made for speed; the other ship was designed to carry cargo. And in light or little winds, she also had the advantage of oars, Daniel explained. Eight men in the very belly of the boat, each handling a great wooden oar that reached out and down into the water through a small hole in the hull, could power the *Mistress* up to a perfectly respectable pace. The lumbering *Mary* would have no hope of escape.

Nate, the thief, hurried past him, then stopped and turned, clearly surprised to see Fish. "You're part of our crew now?"

"A trial. I'm Fish."

"And you fight like one, too," Nate quipped.

Daniel stifled a laugh. "Sorry," he muttered to Fish.

"That was too easy," Nate added. "I hope you prove worthy. We could use more help." Nate looked around to see if anyone was listening, then lowered his voice and leaned in. "Speaking of which, would you mind telling me . . . ah, nothing. Forget about it."

"What?" Fish pressed.

"Well," Nate said, "when I came after you on the docks, was I intimidating?"

Fish wasn't sure how to respond. "I suppose . . ."

"You were terrifying, I'm sure," Daniel added.

"Be honest, Fish," Nate replied.

There was nothing particularly intimidating about the boy now. He'd wrapped a rag around the top of his head and smeared some sort of black gunk beneath his eyes. He looked like an imitation of a pirate, not the real thing. Yet there'd be no harm in telling him what he wanted to hear. "Yes," Fish said after a moment. "Terribly frightening."

"Thanks!" he answered. "Godspeed with the raid today. Remember to keep your cutlass out and your eyes and ears open!"

Nate was off before Fish had a chance to point out that he had no cutlass.

The closest thing he had to a weapon was the swab.

The group sharpening blades called Daniel over to help.

One of the men handed him a dagger; Daniel pointed at something along the edge and passed it back. Apparently, his keen eyesight made him a valued inspector. The girl, Nora, was working alongside them, too, but she was doing the sharpening herself.

Fish continued scrubbing. The mood on the deck grew increasingly tense. Captain Cobb watched from the upper deck at the stern, but Scab was in charge of the details. Walking among the men, he clapped them on their shoulders and backs, handing out pieces of red cloth, which they tied around their arms and heads. When he came to Fish, he stopped, then laughed and walked on.

A pirate Fish hadn't been introduced to yet explained, "We wear the red so we know who is on the other side. It can be hard to see with the smoke. Here," he said, pulling an extra red rag from his pocket, "wrap this around your head to be safe. I wouldn't want to cut you down by accident!"

As Fish tied the rag around his forehead, he noticed Nate approaching Scab. "I want to be one of the boarders," Nate said.

"A boarder? Are you ready for that?"

"Yes, sir," Nate answered. "I'm a good shot, sir, with a quick blade."

In a blur Scab unsheathed his cutlass and swung at Nate. The boy's weapon flashed out, blocking Scab's strike.

"True enough," Scab said. He lowered his blade. "Very

well. You may join the boarding party. If you survive, I'll consider you for a permanent position."

Nate stifled a smile, then hurried off toward the bow.

Fish was going to ask someone just what it meant to be a boarder when he heard a call from high up the mast. All the men turned and stared to the south. The mostly hidden sun was high in the sky, yet the fog was still thick enough to obscure the horizon. There, from within the mist, a massive ship emerged, like a ghost vessel sailing in from some distant, mysterious world.

Scab shouted, "OARS!"

The boat began lurching forward. Fish ran to the railing. Below, four oars were splashing and stroking in unison.

"SAILS!" Scab shouted next.

The wind was light, but as they moved out from the shelter of the cove, the breeze caught the sails, and the *Scurvy Mistress* began to accelerate.

The *Mary* was soon only a short swim away.

Next, he heard Cobb yell. It sounded like he shouted "stomach," but Fish wasn't sure. The next word, though, was clear:

"FIRE!"

A deck-shaking explosion followed. A spinning, smoking cannonball shot through the air toward the *Mary*. Fish's stomach sank. His eyes widened with horror. Were they going to drown all those unarmed, innocent passengers?

The shot splashed down off the boat's bow.

A cheer went up from the deck.

Why were they applauding a miss?

He looked to Daniel, who stood nearby. "A warning shot," his friend explained. "A message to the other crew."

On the port side, facing the frigate, more than a dozen men knelt at the railing, pistols and muskets loaded and ready to fire. Yet the crew of the *Mary* had no intention of returning that initial shot. In fact, as the *Scurvy Mistress* approached, Fish didn't see much of a crew at all. There were only three men above deck.

"What do we do now?" Fish asked Daniel.

"We? My role is to stand watch, looking out for other ships, but you do nothing. Stay as far from the fight as you can. Otherwise, you'll be hurt. Or killed."

The *Scurvy Mistress* drew nearer still. The pirates tensed. An uncomfortable silence fell over them. The three men on the *Mary* stood frozen, seemingly ready to submit. Obviously, these were rational men, thought Fish. They'd measured their own strengths against those of the pirates and decided that a battle would be far from even. To prevent the unnecessary loss of lives, they'd chosen to give up.

Soon, the ships were only thirty feet apart. Moravius and three others tossed huge iron hooks tied to long, thick ropes onto the deck of the other boat. Several more men grabbed the lines and pulled, bringing the two ships closer. A group of pirates remained poised at the railing, pistols and muskets ready. A second line of rogues—the boarders,

Fish guessed, since Nate stood with them now—crouched behind them, ready to rush.

Finally, when only a few feet separated the two boats, the boarders leaped across the gap onto the deck of the *Mary*, screaming and shouting as they charged. And with that, Fish saw that this would not be a peaceful raid.

The crew of the *Mary* did not intend to submit without a struggle.

They had merely waited for the ideal moment to strike.

6

War on the Water

As the boarders brandished their blades and pistols, dozens of the *Mary*'s men burst out from closed doors and hatches, firing guns and swinging steel. Pistol and musket fire boomed in the air. Dark smoke clouded the decks of both ships. There were shouts and screams of all kinds: rage and triumph, pain and desperation. Fish backed himself against the railing, as far from the fight as possible, clutching his swab as if it might protect him.

More pirates rushed across to assist the boarders. The firing intensified, pistols popping constantly. The smoke thickened. Fish's eyes and throat began burning. Showers of splintered wood erupted into the air as musket balls rammed into the decks and rails of both ships. Out of the smoke above his head, a dark brown bottle with a flaming cloth stuffed inside crashed to the floor in front of him. Fire leaped up and spread across a small section of the deck. Fish grabbed a soapy bucket of seawater and doused the flames.

Dousing the fire renewed his resolve.

This was no time to cower in fear.

He had to find the purse.

The captain and Moravius had both stormed forward onto the *Mary*.

The ship hadn't sailed far from the coast; Fish could grab the purse, jump overboard, and swim ashore. Somehow, he'd find his way back to the city. He reached into his pocket, grasped the wooden fish, turned it over a few times.

His eyes nearly closed to block out the smoke, he coughed and moved cautiously at first, to avoid the shards from the shattered bottle, then raced down the length of the ship to the captain's cabin, hurried inside, and closed the door.

The battle sounds were muffled, the air free of smoke.

He breathed slowly, in and out, trying to calm himself.

The cabin was small but regal. There was a dining nook with benches at the stern. Two squat, overstuffed bookcases against one wall, plus a pair of leather chairs and a small desk. To his left, a narrow door led to what he guessed was a small bedroom. There was another, smaller door beside it. A private seat of easement, perhaps? That would be a luxury.

Small but colorful windows lined three of the walls;

they reminded him of church. Several great chests lay about, most of them locked tight, a few overflowing with long strings of pearls and coins. There were numerous paintings, too, all featuring pastoral scenes of farms, cows grazing in green meadows, sheep lazing on hilltops. He would have expected sailing ships and stormy, wind-crazed seas. An odd cabin, certainly. But he wouldn't mind living there himself.

One of the small, colorful windows shattered as a shot burst through.

A painting fell to the floor.

Fish reminded himself to be quick.

The next shot could hit him.

In the back corner of the cabin, half hidden behind a pile of weathered sea chests, Fish spied a collection of coins spread out on the surface of the small desk. Beside them lay the leather purse. His heart thumped in his chest.

He started for the coins, then froze as a warm hand lifted the front of his shirt and held a cold knife to his stomach.

"With a single slice I can see what you ate for lunch today."

Nervously, Fish said the first thing that came to mind. "I didn't have any lunch."

His would-be assailant grabbed his shoulder and spun him around. Melinda stood before him. She was about his height, healthy and strong, with powerful arms and wide hips. Her narrow eyebrows were so fine they could have been painted on. Her cheeks were full and red with life, and she was pointing the knife at his chest.

"You're the new boy," she said. "The swimmer."

"Fish," he replied, his eyes locked on the knife.

"And they neglected to feed you?" she asked.

Fish exhaled. For now, at least, she didn't seem quite so eager to stab him. "Daniel brought me some rolls last night. Terribly hard things, like stones. I had a few more after I woke up on deck—"

"You slept on deck? No one provided you with a hammock? This is an egregious error! A frightful oversight! We're supposed to be running a civilized operation, not a ship full of thoughtless brigands!" Dropping the knife to her side, she sat down heavily in one of the comfortable leather chairs as a second window exploded into shards of green and yellow glass. Fish dropped, covering the back of his head with his hands, but when he looked up, he saw that Melinda hadn't flinched. "That was my favorite pane," she lamented. "Tell me, Fish, what are you doing in my cabin?"

Returning to his feet, Fish avoided glancing at the scattered coins.

Now a small section of the door splintered behind him, hit from the outside by an errant pistol shot. Fish found himself crouching again before he realized he'd even moved. He looked up to see Melinda watching him.

"You're terrified, aren't you?" she asked. "Did you slip in here to hide?"

Fish neglected to answer. He shrugged.

She clapped her hands decisively. "Of course you are! What's this, your second day on the ship? And we're already conducting a raid. Hardly civilized at all! I make it a point to look after the kids in the crew. Daniel, Nate, Nora. So, you'll stay in here with me, Fish, until this brutality has concluded, and we'll have lunch." She hurried over to a closet on the far side of the cabin and opened the door, revealing stacks of small cartons of food: biscuits, crackers, tins of salted fish, cheese, and dried, salted meats. "There is one item in here that Daniel and Nate both adore," she said, shuffling the cartons and tins from shelf to shelf, "but you'll have to spare me a moment or two. I had this all organized yesterday. Walter must have gone through it again."

As she stood with her back to him, Fish studied the coins, then patted the others in his pocket, checking again to be sure he still had them. The coins were far more complex than simple shillings, all full of pictures and symbols and fancy lettering. Each one harbored enough details and figures to fit a painting. Some were bright and polished, others weathered and dark.

He shook his head. He couldn't just stand there studying them—this was his chance! Working hurriedly, Fish silently picked up the coins, dropped them quietly into the leather purse. Melinda was mumbling as she searched. The battle sounds hadn't faded entirely, either. Otherwise, she might have heard him. Over her shoulder, Melinda asked, "How about a few biscuits? These are far better than what you'll get below."

He dashed for the door without answering.

Outside, the smoke had thinned.

The firing had stopped.

Fish dashed across the deck and onto the *Mary*.

The pirates were victorious. A few dozen bleeding and bandaged passengers and sailors huddled together near the *Mary*'s fancily carved railing. Moravius stood watch over these hostages—the distant, muffled shouts suggested most of the pirates and their victims were down below. Drinking from a bottle of wine, Thimble was wrapping the wounded with spare rags. He passed by one of the *Mary*'s sailors, a young man who was bleeding from a blow to his head, when Cobb called out to him. "All of the wounded, Thimble, not merely our own."

The red-faced pirate snorted, rolled his small eyes, took another swig, and returned to the bleeding sailor. Nearby, a rotund, bearded man, kneeling on the floor, pleaded for the rogues to leave him alone. Instead of granting his request, Scab calmly walloped him with the butt of his pistol. The man crumpled.

Another passenger protested. Nate rushed over and lifted his own pistol to strike him, but before he could bring the weapon down, Cobb grabbed his wrist, then stared hard into the boy's eyes. "We are not animals. Victory is ours. We will collect our bounty and go."

Go.

Fish had been so enraptured by the scene that he'd forgotten to flee.

He was supposed to be escaping, not standing there gawking.

He hurried to the side of the ship closest to the shore.

If he jumped, someone might hear him, so he lifted one leg over the railing, planning to climb down quietly into the water.

The deck exploded mere inches from his right foot.

A shot meant for someone else, he hoped.

He swung the other leg over.

A second shot followed, striking the railing beside his hand.

"Where do you think you're going, thief?"

He turned to find Melinda, her face as red as her hair, stomping forward over the deck and aiming twin pistols at his chest. The other pirates turned to face him. A sickening feeling spread outward from his center. Not fear, exactly, but something closer to disappointment. A great, heavy, sinking weight in his soul. There was no hope now—he'd never be able to return the coins. He'd failed his uncle. His family, too. He could hardly look at Melinda, either. She'd been kind to him, and he'd cheated her. Fish felt terrible. About everything. He wanted to dive off that boat and disappear.

Hands shaking, he tossed the purse, which landed at her feet.

Cobb rushed to her side. Moravius, too.

Before either could say a word, though, a new threat arose.

"Captain!" Daniel shouted. "Another ship is approaching!"

"Navy?"

"No," Daniel said. "A sloop. Fine and fast, from the looks of her. New, bright white sails. She's a good distance away but gaining."

Melinda flashed Fish a last sneer before eyeing the boat herself. "That ship was in the harbor," she noted.

Fish squinted. The ship was too far away for him to be certain, but it looked like the fine vessel tied fast to the docks where he'd first spotted Reginald Swift.

"You're mistaken," Scab replied. "I'd have seen her myself."

"Another raid?" Thimble suggested.

"Let her be," Scab snapped.

"Is your hunger for battle sated?" Cobb asked.

"We've had enough fight today," the pirate growled.

Cobb paused, obviously surprised by his normally war-hungry first mate's suggestion. Then he turned to the crew. "Transfer what bounty you can and hoist the sails!

We've been sailing these crowded waters too long. The time has come for us to cross the blue desert and venture into friendlier seas!"

A cheer rang out at the announcement.

The blue desert? He had to mean the ocean. At the railing, Fish looked over his shoulder. What was he supposed to do? He could still flee. He could find his way home, or find his mother's family, at least. But if he was going to escape, it would have to be now.

Unfortunately, the captain grabbed him by his too-large shirt before he could make his decision. "Oh no, boy," Cobb said. "You're not slithering off. You have questions to answer."

7

Walk the Plank

The *Scurvy Mistress* sailed away, leaving the battered *Mary*, her passengers, and the mystery sloop in her wake. Any hope of completing his task was now gone. And Fish had been so close! Even if he could somehow find his way back to Uncle Gerry, he'd probably lose his position. He'd be sent home, surely. His brothers would wallop him. Would Roisin or his sisters even talk to him?

He refused to return home a failure. In fact, Fish was not going anywhere. Cobb had ordered a pirate named Knot to bind him to the railing, and the man had done so with amazing speed and dexterity. Daniel checked on Fish, but when he explained what he'd done, his friend was beyond disappointed. "What were you thinking, Fish?" he asked. "Have you been listening at all? Or have you been drinking seawater? If there's one person you need to respect, it's the captain. And you stole from his cabin!"

"I was *not* stealing," Fish insisted.

Daniel shook his head and walked off.

As the ship sailed on, the crew sorted through and recorded the various trinkets, coins, and treasures plundered from the *Mary*. The men stood in a line, their pockets stuffed, some of them carrying or carting small chests, and one by one handed their haul to an old, gray-haired, blade-thin man with an unusually long head. He studied each item closely, then handed it to one of a pair of pirates behind him, who stored everything in a collection of small barrels. Fish watched for a long while.

"That's Foot."

The sun had just burned through the clouds, and the glare made it difficult to see, but from the voice, Fish knew it was Daniel. "He's the purser?" Fish guessed.

"Correct. He's a right wizard with numbers. Notice how he doesn't even keep a ledger?"

That was odd, Fish thought. Usually the pursers he dealt with around the docks had a pad and pencil on hand.

"Has no need for one." Daniel tapped his head. "Keeps it all up here. We call him Foot because his right foot is probably the foulest-smelling thing on the ocean. He's been wearing the same boot for decades. The left one he changes three or four times a year, but not the right one. He says it helps him think. And it might, given the fact that he's always tapping it when he's adding up numbers, like a fiddler keeping a beat. Always the right foot, never the left."

Daniel was right; the man's right foot, shod in a heavily worn brown boot, was practically bouncing on the deck.

Now Daniel leaned against the railing beside him; his tone changed. "You've probably got it better than Nate the Great. He did the only thing worse than swiping something off the captain."

"What's that?"

"He stole from the crew. During the raid, he grabbed a few armfuls of loot but tried to keep a necklace for himself. Didn't hand it to Foot when his turn came. Can't figure out why, either, since the thing didn't look to be worth all that much—merely a bit of silver with a few cheap stones."

"Why is he being punished if it wasn't worth anything?" Fish asked.

"Why?! It's against our rules, our code, our entire way of life! You really haven't been listening, have you? When we take a prize, everything, and I mean every last trinket, from a golden bracelet to an old silver fork, goes to Foot, who divides it up, all of it, among the crew."

Watching the purser, and the line of pirates before him, Fish thought about this for a moment. "So that necklace was as much yours as it was his?"

"Right! Cobb isn't too happy. I think he had some faith in Nate. Thought he'd make a good captain one day. But rules are rules."

"What are they going to do to him?" Fish asked. Daniel pointed toward the bow, where the men had begun to convene as the last of them deposited their hauls with Foot. Cobb and Moravius remained near the stern, unwilling or unable to watch. "Daniel? What are they going to do to Nate?"

The young pirate pulled a medallion out from under his shirt, kissed it twice quickly, then said, "They're making him walk the plank."

Fish looked back over his shoulder. The coast wasn't too far. "Won't he swim to shore?"

"Pirates don't swim, remember?" Daniel answered. "Walking the plank is a death sentence."

Death? Fish felt suddenly cold. He understood the importance of rules, but death? That seemed like an unjustly permanent punishment for such a small theft.

A group of pirates pushed a narrow but long plank of wood through a short opening beneath the railing on the far side of the ship. They secured one end by rolling a heavy barrel on top. The other end stretched out several long paces from the side of the boat and hung over the sea. A man who was bald but for a horseshoe of brown hair that wrapped around his head from ear level down dragged Nate up onto the deck from below. Scab and Thimble watched smiling. Nate shook himself free of the other man's grip. He paused near the railing, walked to the edge of the board, out over the deep water, then spun to face the crew.

Scab, stifling laughter, shouted, "Any last words?"

Nate gulped. "I had my reasons for taking the necklace," he began in a quivering voice. "I'd meant it to be a gift." Fish noticed Nate's gaze shift to the back of the crowd. Nora was standing there, dressed in a ragged, dirty blouse and loose, mismatched pants. When Nate looked at her, she lowered her head. "But I was wrong," he continued. "Wrong to steal from my family."

"Not very bright, either," replied Thimble. "You could've bought the lass a necklace with your share!"

A few of the pirates chuckled, but several more men averted their eyes, as if they were too pained to watch what was going to happen next.

Finally, Nate said, "I accept my fate," and leaped backward into the sea.

Daniel lifted the medallion to his lips and kissed it twice more.

There was a loud splash, and then Fish heard Nate thrashing at the surface. Thimble, Scab, and a few others leaned over the railing, pointing and laughing. Nate was gasping for air and swallowing water. Fish struggled against the ropes. The bindings loosened—for once, he was thankful of his small hands. Fish pulled harder at the knots. The skin of his wrists was burning. Yet he forced one hand out, then the next, and without hesitation, he sprang to the railing and then off and into the water below. He swam deep, beneath the hull, and surfaced on the far side as the doomed young pirate began to sink. Fish raced to

Nate, slipped his arm across the half-drowned boy's chest, and held him faceup, allowing him to breathe. Nate was coughing, but safe.

The pirates on deck were thoroughly confused.

"You can't save him!" one of the rogues yelled.

"That's not allowed!"

"Let him drown!" another pirate added.

Yet a few other crew members cheered. Then Cobb came to the railing. "Bring them up!" he ordered. "Bring them both up."

A rope ladder was dropped down into the water. Fish swam Nate to it, breathing heavily from the strain. Still coughing, confused that he wasn't dead and drowned, Nate gripped the rope and slowly climbed. Fish waited, then started to follow the boy. Halfway up, he looked back toward the shore. A fog had gathered along the coast, and he could no longer see the beach.

Ireland was disappearing from view.

8

Your Family Now

Inside the captain's cabin, Fish shivered. His pants and shirt were soaked. His forearms were tied roughly to the hard wooden armrests of his chair. Cobb and Melinda were watching him and whispering as Moravius swept the broken glass from the floor. The shattered window had already been covered up with a wooden board. Fish felt his teeth begin to chatter. Begrudgingly, Melinda spread a wool blanket over his shaking legs. Cobb puffed intensely on a tobacco pipe. The giant looked pensive, too, but Fish wasn't sure what someone who made rooster noises could be thinking.

"You tried to steal from us," Cobb said.

"You betrayed my trust!" Melinda added.

"I had a responsibility—"

"Yes, yes, we've heard all about that," Cobb said. "I

applaud your sense of responsibility and your loyalty. Both respectable qualities. But your loyalties are supposed to lie with me and my crew. And now this rescue! What were you thinking?"

"Saving Nate was the right thing to do," Fish protested.

"And the wrong time to do it!" Melinda replied.

"We're at a perilous juncture," Cobb added. "We need to maintain order! Nate was condemned to walk the plank. He accepted his fate."

"He did walk the plank," Fish noted. "I only grabbed him afterward."

"You think you're the first noble soul on a pirate ship?" Cobb asked. "Your friend Daniel tried something like that once. Tried to push the plank overboard so one of the men wouldn't have to walk. Scab walloped him so hard he can hardly hear out of his right ear."

A circular rack of tobacco pipes sat on Cobb's desk. He spun it, watching the pipe stems turn. "How do I know you're not a spy?"

Fish laughed. "A spy? Are you serious?"

"You snuck into our cabin," Cobb said.

"But I was—"

"You've been working for one of our chief competitors, a very famous and successful treasure hunter, a Mr. Reginald Swift."

"Reginald Swift is a treasure hunter?"

"Do not play the part of simpleton with us. Tell me now: Do you work directly for Mr. Swift and his fiendish mother?"

"The Swifts? No!"

"Who is your employer?"

Former employer would be more accurate—Uncle Gerry would never give him his old position back. "Reidy Merchants," he answered.

"Known traffickers of treasure-related information," Melinda replied.

Again, Fish laughed. Of all the accusations, this one had to be the most absurd. "That's ridiculous," he said.

"Ridiculous?" Cobb replied. "A goat dressed in an evening gown is ridiculous."

"Or a cat with spectacles," Melinda added.

The giant grumbled oddly.

"Precisely!" Cobb replied. "Why would a cat wear spectacles? That is ridiculous. Very clever, my dear."

"Uncle Gerry is a simple merchant," Fish insisted. "He's not the sort to be involved with pirates and treasure hunters." And yet his uncle had given him that purse. He'd sent him to meet the Swifts. Could what they were saying be true?

"A simple merchant? Ha! You are wrong. Incorrect! Mistaken! Those coins are a critical clue—"

The giant coughed and scratched his large, crooked nose. Cobb stopped mid-sentence. He rubbed his head and his thick curls moved in unison. Fish hadn't realized he was wearing a wig.

"Never mind the coins," Cobb continued. "Your behavior suggests you are not to be trusted."

Surely his rescue of Nate meant something. And he'd helped Scab, too. "I saved two of your crew from drowning! Why would I do that if I was a spy?"

"To sow the seeds of mutiny!" Cobb responded. "A ship like ours can only function if all the men—"

"And women."

"—and *women* aboard agree to adhere to a set of rules. If the crew suspects that our rules are not carved into the very hull of this ship, they will bend, circumvent, and break them. If anyone were to find out that you broke into our cabin and we let you live . . ."

The captain's wig slipped slightly; he fidgeted with it for a moment, then stopped, satisfied. Fish caught Melinda rolling her eyes. "Yes," she added, "but you were the one who decided that Nate could live after he saved him."

"The rules say thieves must walk the plank. Nathaniel did exactly that." Holding out the stem of his pipe, the captain added, "The rules don't say he has to die."

"Then you can't blame our young spy here for having a heart."

"Whose side are you on? Mine or the spy's?"

"I'm not a spy!" Fish declared. If his arms were free, he would've slammed down a fist for emphasis. "I saved him because it's cruel to let someone drown over a necklace. Nate made a mistake. He apologized. That should have been enough!" He waited for them to respond. They remained silent, staring at him. "I'd rather walk the plank myself than be part of a crew that lets someone drown over a bauble . . ."

Now he waited. They were quiet. Had he pushed too far?

"Young man," Cobb responded, his tone softening, "I would prefer it if we never raided another ship. Unfortunately, this would all but ensure mutiny. If the men do not accumulate riches at a steady pace, my control of the *Scurvy Mistress* will not endure very long."

"You're the captain," Fish replied. "Don't they have to do as you say?"

"On a traditional vessel, perhaps," Cobb answered. "But a pirate ship is a different sort of society, boy. The captain is only in control for as long as the majority of the crew desires."

"What happens if they don't want you to be captain anymore?"

"With hope we will never discover that," Melinda replied.

"For now, I hold sway over most of these rogues. Their interests are aligned with mine. Yet a number of our sailors, and a handful of very valuable and useful ones at that, lack the patience for the sort of quest I prefer. They need to be appeased with raids and robberies of the kind we conducted today."

"Like Scab?" Fish asked.

"Yes."

Fish glanced around the room. "You already have quite a store of jewels here . . ."

"Trinkets," Cobb said. "We seek far grander treasures."

Grander? Fish couldn't help imagining his own chest full of gold and jewels. The coins would shine like the surface of a sunstruck lake. Strings of white pearls would lie coiled beneath green emeralds as big as his fists. He'd send his riches home to provide for his family. That is, assuming he received a fair portion. "Does everyone share in these treasures?" he asked.

"Not evenly, but yes, of course. Even our youngest members receive a portion of a share."

"Would that be enough to buy a horse?"

Cobb and Melinda laughed; the giant smiled, too.

"A herd of horses, my boy!" Cobb answered.

The captain struck a match. He re-fired his pipe, sucked in deeply, and puffed out the thick smoke. Fish watched the gray cloud rise and spread along the ceiling. What was he to do now? Even if he could swim to shore, Uncle Gerry wouldn't have him. His parents might welcome him home, but he didn't want to return to the farm ragged and penniless. No, they'd sent him away to earn money. They'd placed their faith in him. He would not disappoint them.

Fish was certain the life of a seafaring adventurer would be more difficult and dangerous than that of a messenger. But he'd already made one friend in Daniel, which was more than he had in the city. And a few days in this life had already been far more exciting than anything he'd experienced before.

Yes, he was sure of it. Never mind the purse and the Swifts. He'd join the crew. He would not buy his family one horse, but a herd!

First, though, he had to convince Cobb and the others that they could trust him. "I'm sorry," he said at last. "I shouldn't have snuck in here. I shouldn't have tried to take back the purse. Especially since you were being so kind, Melinda."

She nodded. "I'm not sure a simple apology will suffice, no matter how sincere. How can we be certain that we can trust you?"

Fish thought of the last of the coins, and the small, carved fish in his pocket. The wood had become smoother in the months since Roisin had given it to him; he rubbed it constantly for comfort. Giving it up would hurt deeply, but he had to show them he was devoted. "There are a few things in my pockets I'd like you to have," Fish said. "Can you grab them?"

Skeptical, Melinda held a knife in her left hand and removed the coins, then the wooden fish, with her right. She glared at the coins first.

"They fell out of the purse when Nate stole it on the pier," Fish explained.

The navigator looked to Cobb, then Moravius, with excitement.

Next, she eyed the wooden fish curiously before flicking it to Cobb. The captain inspected it briefly. He was unimpressed. "And this?"

"My sister gave it to me when I left home for the city," Fish explained. "I know it isn't much. It doesn't compare to these treasures you have here. But it's my single and most valuable possession. It reminds me of my family, and I'm giving it to you because what's mine is now yours."

Cobb glanced at his wife and the giant, then smiled. In two frighteningly fast motions, Melinda sliced free the ropes that had bound Fish's wrists to the chair. Then Cobb tossed him the carving. "We're your family now," the captain pronounced. "Welcome aboard, Fish."

9

Hell's Kitchen

A bell chimed, and Cobb ordered Fish belowdecks for his dinner. Although the place still frightened him, he descended on the command from his new captain. The pirates ate and slept in a single large cabin that ran nearly the length of the ship. Against both walls, huge black cannons sat secured by thick ropes. Hammocks hung from the ceiling. The wood was black and green with mold, and the stench assaulted his nose like a shot from one of the cannons. Fish did have experience with revolting smells. He'd shoveled and stepped in gargantuan piles of cow manure and once spent several months tending to the family's three foul pigs. Yet this room . . . he could find no word to describe the singular potency of its smell.

There must have been two dozen men packed inside. Some of the pirates stood; some sat on the floor in groups of five or six, eating from small bowls and drinking from dented metal mugs. The air was hot and thick, the noise incredibly loud, as if an entire city had been stuffed into a single room.

Noah, a bearded, potbellied pirate he'd learned about earlier, waddled toward him. He was small and dark-skinned, with a pencil tucked behind one ear and nails behind the other. Noah was the ship's carpenter, which meant he was perpetually fixing cracks and leaks and splits in the aging wooden vessel. Daniel said that Cobb believed Noah's carpentry skills matched those of the Bible's famed boatbuilder, and he was a man of verse, too. Daniel had mentioned that he could write a shanty in under ten seconds. Fish flinched as Noah dropped an oversize hand on his shoulder. "Welcome," he said. "Putrocious, isn't it?"

"I don't know—"

"Of course you don't! It's my own word. A combination of 'putrid' and 'atrocious.' I believe no other combination of letters in the English language quite captures the stench down here, so I had to invent a word." Noah leaned in and smiled. "You survived your first raid. Congratulations."

"Thank you," Fish replied.

"Frightening bunch, aren't they?" Noah said, waving his arm toward the men. "That group there"—Noah pointed to a circle of rogues—"calls themselves the Ravenous Rovers. Their main goal in this waterlogged life is to see to it that their bellies are filled with salted meats. Their leader is Sammy the Stomach—"

"The gunner, right?"

"That's right," Noah said. "His appetite is unmatched. Even names his guns after food." Noah nodded toward one of the cannons. "Calls that six-pounder Meat Pie because she minces the decks of opposing ships."

"Six-pounder?"

"That means she shoots a six-pound shot. An eight fires an eight," Noah explained. The pirate subtly pointed around the room as he introduced the other groups. "The Tea Leaves, those well-dressed fellows in the corner, they're all British, ex–Royal Navy men. You'd do well to sit with the Over and Unders, the gents working with the ropes. You might learn a trick or two about their trade. But I'd avoid the Ancient Eight, those old-timers huddled on the starboard side. All they do is complain about their ailments."

Quickly, Fish counted the members of the group. "There's only three of them . . ."

Noah shrugged. "We've lost a few over the years. As I said, they're ancient."

Daniel was sitting with the Over and Unders, and Fish recognized Knot, the man who'd tied him up. Behind them, in a larger group, Fish spotted Scab and Thimble, the fancily dressed tailor. He didn't need to ask about that portion of the crew. Any pirate sitting with Scab was not to be trusted.

Someone tapped Fish on the shoulder—Nate. The boy stared at the deck as he muttered a brief and barely audible, "Thank you."

He hurried off before Fish could even think of a reply.

"We're a charming bunch, aren't we?" Noah joked. "Well, there's your brief introduction to our little paradise." He pointed toward a small counter. "Now go and get your grub before it's gone."

A few men waited in the line, each holding a bowl. Nora stood on the other side of the counter, inside the small galley, ladling what looked like soup out of a large pot. Fish said a quick prayer that no one would strike him as he crossed the crowded room and hurried, head down, to the counter. The line had shrunk to nothing. Nora nodded to him. Her eyes were a very familiar shade of green—the color of a pasture in spring. He'd never seen eyes so odd. He was stunned.

She leaned forward. "Nice rescue," she whispered.

"Thanks," he said. "I'm Fish."

"I know," she replied. "I'm Nora. Well, Fish, what would you like to eat?"

Finally, he felt his fortunes turning. An actual meal! But what did he want? Beef? A roasted chicken? Either would do, but some nice, thick brown bread with butter and a few warm potatoes would be ideal. A glass of milk, too. "What are my choices?"

Nora lifted the lid of the large, blackened pot behind

the counter to reveal a steaming grayish-green sludge. "You have two choices. Gruel, and gruel with hardtack."

"Hardtack?"

"Biscuits, baked nearly before you and I were born. Hard as stones if you bite into them plain, but if you break them up a bit, crumble them into your gruel, and mix them around, they might not crack any of your teeth."

Fish gulped. "Do you have any butter?"

"Yes, let me just . . ." She ducked behind the counter, then popped up again. "Ha! Had you, didn't I? Butter? We don't have butter on the *Mistress*. Not for you, anyway. That's a luxury. The diet here is simple, really. Gruel and hardtack at night. A piece of meat once a day, and some hard cheese, too. Gruel and a glass of goat's milk in the morning—"

"You have goats on board?"

"Yes, and hens, too, all down below this deck. You might even get an egg one day." Nora stopped stirring and studied Fish for a moment. "Look at you," she said. "Pale, smooth skin." She reached over the counter and took his hands; he shivered. "Palms that have never seen true toil. Eyes that haven't witnessed the dark side of the world. Let me guess. Your accent is Irish. Grew up in Dublin, I presume? Attended a fancy school, waited on by servants? Then you ran away from home for a life of adventure and found yourself here, wishing you'd never left."

Fish pulled his hands away. He closed them into fists. "What do you mean I've never seen the dark side of the world? I lived in a city. And at least three times in the past two days, someone has pressed a knife to my skin. I didn't attend a fancy school, either." He paused for a long breath. "I was raised on a farm and sent off to work because Shamrock—that's our horse—died. Now I'm here, hoping to earn my share and do what I can to help my family."

Nora held up her hands, palms out. "I meant no offense, Fish."

He exhaled. Whether she meant to insult him or not, he didn't appreciate being regarded as an innocent child. There was more to him than that—and he would show her. He'd show all of them.

His stomach grumbled.

He'd show them later. After he ate.

"Before I can help anyone, though," Fish continued, "I really need food. So, whether it's plain gruel or gruel with crack-your-teeth biscuit, I would very much appreciate it if you would serve me some." He took another extended breath before adding, "Please."

Nora's head pitched forward. "What did you say?"

"I said I'm hungry and—"

"No," she said, waving her hand, "after that."

"'Please'?"

"That's right! You did say it! 'Please'!" A smile lit up

her face. "Please!" she repeated. "No one around here ever says 'please'!"

Suddenly Daniel appeared beside Fish. "Seriously, Nora? I always say please and thank you. Nate does, too."

She dismissed his protest. "But you're my friends, Daniel. Of course you two say please. This odd bird here is a stranger with manners." Fish considered objecting and noting that he was not a bird, but then she passed him a bowl. Daniel playfully flicked a piece of hardtack at Nora and walked off. Fish dropped in the hardened biscuit and spooned some of the gruel into his mouth. The texture of it was unpleasant—more muddy than creamy—and it had an unexpected tang that suggested at least one of the ingredients had spoiled. Yet he swallowed one spoonful after another. Fish tried to imagine he was eating one of his mother's stews, with fresh potatoes and vegetables. This improved the experience briefly. Then the thought of those meals brought up a chain of memories: of his mother, of his sisters and brothers, and of how his father looked at him when he left him with Uncle Gerry. His father loved him. Fish knew that. His father didn't want to leave him in the city—he simply had no choice. The thought of home shook Fish. Had he made the right decision? Perhaps he should have jumped off the ship when he had the chance.

Fish clenched his teeth. He was almost twelve years

old. He had responsibilities. He had to show his family, this girl, and the rest of the crew that he was strong. That he was prepared for what life on the ocean was going to blow his way.

Meanwhile, Nora was watching him. Right—the gruel. Was she hoping for a compliment? Fish thought hard, searching his mind for something nice to say. "Ummm . . . it's warm . . . and filling?"

"I can see you're not impressed, but it's not my fault. It's the ingredients. I actually like cooking. Don't mind fighting, either. Thankfully Cobb and Melinda let me do a little of both."

"You actually like fighting?"

Nora shrugged. "It's not that I want to hurt anyone. It's just that I've developed some skill and might as well contribute to the crew. I'm far more effective than most of these booze-brained beasts. Here," she said, "watch."

Across the cabin, one of the Ravenous Rovers was lifting a sodden piece of hardtack out of his gruel. Nora exhaled, removed a knife from her sleeve, lifted it up next to her ear, and flung it across the room in one rapid flick.

The knife spun end over end, spearing the biscuit when it was only inches from the pirate's foul mouth, then jammed into a post. Now the scalawag held only a small piece of hardtack in his hand. He popped this into his mouth, turned toward Nora. She winked. The pirate smiled crookedly. Then he reached over, removed the knife and the soaked biscuit, and brought the former back to Nora, nodding humbly as he laid it on the counter.

"I'll give him an extra serving at the next meal," Nora whispered. "That little display wasn't just for you, either. Melinda encourages me to remind the men every so often that I'm not one to be bothered." Nora showed him a knife tucked up her right sleeve, then a second and third strapped to her ankles. She slipped the recently returned blade into another hidden sheath. "I mastered the art of throwing them all by myself." She shrugged, then whispered, "Of course, I could also poison any one pirate's food, so very few of them are ignorant enough to give me any trouble." She stopped; Fish was staring at her. "Don't worry," Nora added with a smile. She reached out and patted him on the shoulder. "I won't poison you, Fish. Not unless you give me a reason."

10

Conundrum in the Cabin

Three weeks passed. The heaving and swaying of the wave-rocked boat had left him feeling sick for days. The food was terrible, the drinking water foul. Fish lost all sense of time. When he finally asked one of the men what day it was, he realized that he'd missed his birthday. He'd turned twelve without even knowing it.

Just before dawn each morning, he awoke to the rooster-like call of Moravius. The pirates would swing out of their hammocks, fold and hook them to the ceiling, stretch and growl, belch and cough, then stomp up to the deck. The pirate with the horseshoe of hair, a friend of Scab called Jumping Jack, often led them through a series of exercises and stretches. The captain believed it kept them fit.

Next came the work. Fish was left with the hideous, vile, stomach-turning task of washing the "seats of ease-ment" three times a day, but the vast majority of his time was devoted to swabbing the decks. Daniel and Nate busied themselves with all types of small tasks, and Daniel did plenty of writing in his new notebook, too. Most of what he jotted down seemed to be details about life on the ship, but one spread of pages was a mix of letters rearranged to form different words. When Fish had asked him what he was working on, though, Daniel had closed the book and put it away. All he'd say was that it involved a little project for the captain—one he had to keep secret.

Fish wished he had a private project of his own. Instead, for hours and hours each day, he simply pushed the swab back and forth upon the wood. The smooth skin of his palms and fingers turned red and raw. Nora would lend him rags to wrap around his hands for protection, and although they hardly helped, he appreciated her kindness. She didn't poison him, either, which was nice.

He despised the swab for the pain it caused, but it also earned him respect. In the crew's cabin, he scrubbed away what seemed to be centuries-old grime and slime, revealing handsome, richly grained wood. Sammy the Stomach claimed he'd been sleeping better at night with the floor beneath his hammock so clean. Noah lauded him for respecting the grain of the wood. Men would come down to grab a few lengths of line or some other supplies, smack Fish on the back, and bellow praise. "Well done, boy!" "She'll be a new ship when you're finished!"

When the crew said the trip across the ocean would take

six weeks, it sounded like an eternity, but the days raced by. Fish sometimes became so lost in his work that the chimes for mealtime, rung six hours apart, would sound after what felt like a few minutes. Their labors ceased not long after dark. To help educate Fish about their peculiar world, Daniel would lecture him on deck, under the bright stars. Other members of the crew often listened alongside Fish— Daniel was a sought-after expert on pirate stories, and Nora, an equally skilled teller of tales, would sometimes join him. If the moon was bright enough, Daniel would read something from his collection of papers, including the single-page broadsides sold in cities that told of the adventures of the world's most feared and notorious rogues.

Before long, though, the lessons would be interrupted by the singing, fighting, or card-playing of their crewmates. Late into the evening, the pirates would laugh and croon in loud, rumbling voices, rarely in unison. Thanks to Noah, there was a song to match almost every occasion. Whenever a fight erupted, for example, they'd sing:

> *Well, here we go with another row,*
> *Two pirates fighting for power.*
> *This one's fierce with his fists for sure,*
> *But that one hits like a flower.*

The fights were as much a part of the ship as its sails. Fish tried to intervene on several occasions, suggesting that the combatants might be better off discussing their disagreement, but he'd invariably find himself flicked out of the scrum like an insignificant gnat. One evening, not too long into the trip, Daniel convinced him to abandon these attempts. "You can't reason with rum," he said.

Eventually the men would go below, unfurl their hammocks, climb inside, and sleep. According to Scab, Fish didn't deserve his own hammock, so he slept on some ragged sections of old sails. For the first few nights, he'd rested his head on a clump of cabbage wrapped in cloth. When Melinda discovered this misguided invention, however, she tossed the wilting greens overboard. "Do you want vermin nibbling near your ears all night?" she'd asked. No, he did not, and he was very thankful when she taught him how to carefully roll a length of sail into a surprisingly comfortable pillow.

Some of the pirates slept like stones. Others constantly turned and even cried out. There were stretches of silence, too, but these were worse, as Fish would hear the patter of little rodent feet as they crept out of hiding in search of food. Once, he watched a rat crawl up and onto Scab's thick beard, where it nibbled at the crumbs left there from dinner. The vile scalawag pleasantly stroked its furry back without waking.

Many of the men were sleepwalkers. Fish was no stranger to this phenomenon: His brother Conor was a particularly skilled sleep-worker. On more than one occasion, someone in the family awoke in the morning to find Conor lying flat in the field, his hands dirty from working the soil as he dreamed. But Fish had never seen two people sleepwalking in the same room, and on the *Scurvy Mistress* that became a common sight. Noah and Sammy the Stomach twice walked into each other without waking. Jumping Jack often swung out of his hammock and exercised with his eyes closed, and the Ravenous Rovers would sometimes line up at the kitchen counter, their hands bearing imaginary bowls, waiting in their sleep for food that never arrived.

One night, when the crew was quiet and the rats had not yet snuck out of the shadows, Fish found that he couldn't sleep, so he ventured up to the deck for a quiet communion with the night sky. Outside, Bat—who earned his name because he slept during the day and worked all through the night—manned the tiller. The sharp-eyed pirate known as Owl, another nocturnal worker, sat at his usual place atop the mast, scanning the dark horizon. The moon was bright. The scene was so calm, so peaceful, that Fish considered sleeping right there on deck . . . then he heard Daniel.

"Stand back, dragon," Daniel mumbled. "You'll not breathe your deadly fire on Daniel the Dragonslayer."

Then he swung a wooden sword hard against a barrel.

Fish heard Bat and Owl laughing.

"It's a habit of his," Owl called down. "Noah carved

him a wooden sword for this very purpose. Usually he grabs a real one, and one of us switches it out."

"Now he can fight all the sleep dragons he wants without hurting himself or anyone else," Bat added. "Don't wake him, Fish. It's entertaining."

The next morning, Fish was sitting at breakfast with the Over and Unders, learning about the intricacies of obscure knots, when Scab bellowed his name. He threw up his hands, expecting to be hit. Instead, Scab demanded to know what he'd been doing up on deck so late the previous night. Fish claimed he simply had trouble sleeping.

"Couldn't sleep? Then I suppose we're not working you hard enough. I apologize. From now on, you will be on night duty in addition to your labors during the day."

Fish nearly choked on his spoonful of gruel. "What about sleep?"

Scab clapped him hard on the back. "You'll manage. There's always scrubbing to do."

Noah, who was eating nearby, pulled out a pencil and said, "That would make a nice chorus." Then he coughed and intoned:

Sailing across the ocean blue
There's always scrubbing to do.

Not one for singing, Scab raised his hand as if he were going to strike the songwriter. Noah flinched, fumbled

86

with the pencil behind his ear, and promptly turned back to his breakfast. As he stomped away, Scab smacked his cutlass down onto the rim of Fish's bowl, spilling his last few mouthfuls of gruel onto the deck. "Clean that up, too," he growled.

The rest of the day passed uneventfully, and that night after dinner, Bat, who had just woken up, approached Fish. "Good morning!" he said. "Time for work."

The deck was wet and cold, the work pointless. He'd spent all day swabbing, so there was nothing left to clean. After an hour, he decided it might be a good idea to lie down and rest his head on a coil of rope—just for a moment. His eyes were beginning to give in to the fatigue when he heard a curse.

"That man!" Melinda shouted. "That man will put me in my grave!"

Fish shook his head, grabbed his swab, and walked back toward the cabin.

He found Melinda pacing and mumbling to herself.

"What man?" he asked. Then, in a whisper, he added, "Scab?"

Melinda glared at him. Fish had a strong sense of when someone needed to talk. He recalled how his mother used to have such moments. What he learned from those experiences was that his mother simply needed someone to listen to her sometimes. He wondered if Melinda was similar.

"No, I'm not talking about Scab," she answered

after a pause. She squinted at the swab in his hand. "Are you *working*?"

"Scab ordered me—"

She grabbed the handle and tossed the swab aside. "We'll have a talk with Scab," she said. "But never mind him for a moment. Tell me, Fish, what do you think of our captain?"

Fish watched the waves for a moment before answering. "I respect him," he said at last. "He seems more . . . thoughtful than the other men. More controlled. Whenever he appears poised to pop, he traces that scar on his chin and settles himself."

"You noticed that? How observant!"

"Why does he do that?" Fish asked.

"A reminder. He has a temper, believe me. And he could not control it so well in his youth. Long before I met him, he engaged in a duel with a man who'd once been a good friend. His friend left him with that scar, and in self-defense, your captain was forced to take the man's life. The death still haunts him, and that scar reminds him that violence—even when it seems necessary—often leads to undesirable ends."

A silence fell between them, and then Melinda slapped her palm down on a railing. "We've drifted," she said, and she wasn't speaking of the ship. "I believe you were wondering why I'm angry? I'll tell you. I'm angry because the leader of our enterprising band can be such a selfish, pompous, arrogant—"

"Fool?" Cobb asked. The captain was standing outside the cabin with his balding, wigless head exposed. "Or would you prefer to call me an imbecile? Tell me, Melinda, what choice names had you planned next?"

Even in the darkness, Fish could see her round face redden. "'Imbecile' is perfect, actually," she replied. "Or maybe Noah could invent something better."

Fish picked up his swab and slowly started to edge away.

Cobb began speaking in a near whisper. "How could you call me selfish?" he asked. "How many times must I tell you that I'm doing this for us? If we succeed, we can live the life we've always wanted."

"That doesn't mean you can treat me like one of your crew until we find it! Mind your behavior."

"I'm trying!" Cobb continued, lowering his voice. "But I have an entire crew counting on me to lead them to riches, and we're no closer to solving the puzzle than we were when we first grabbed the coins! Perhaps you'd like me to step aside and let someone else lead the search? Who would you propose?" He waved his arms around. "Ah yes, what about you, Fish? Perhaps you could solve our grand conundrum in the cabin?"

Fish was not ready to solve anything. He was ready to be somewhere else. Anywhere else. An hour sniffing Foot's yellowing toes or inhaling Scab's ripe breath would have been preferable to another minute stuck between these two.

"Maybe he could," Melinda countered. "He's certainly resourceful. Clever enough, too."

"Fine," Cobb answered. "Bring him inside."

The captain, fuming, returned to the cabin. Melinda looked at the door, then at Fish, who was thoroughly confused. "What just happened?" Fish asked. "What's a conun . . ."

"Conundrum. An unnecessarily formal word. He's talking about a puzzle."

"You want me to solve a puzzle?"

"Not just any puzzle. One that may reveal the location of a great treasure." Melinda placed a comforting hand on his shoulder. "Don't worry, Fish. He doesn't really expect you to find the answer. Would you grant me a favor, though?"

Fish agreed, unsure of how else to respond.

"Prove him wrong."

11

Secrets in the Coins

In the center of the cabin, the coins that had caused all his troubles were spread across the table. Cobb motioned to them grandly. "So?"

So? How was he supposed to know what to do? Cobb acted as if Fish could simply look at the coins and solve their puzzle. Melinda was watching him expectantly, too. Even the giant, who had dropped his monstrous frame into a seat in the corner, appeared interested. The captain slid a chair toward the edge of the table. Fish sat and pulled himself forward. Twelve of the coins were gold, others silver, still others the color of rust. The discs varied in thickness and size, too. A few were no bigger than his thumbnail, while most were three or four times as large. Some were chipped at the edges, irregularly shaped. He started to count them and tallied forty-one in all. He moved the twelve gold coins away from the others. Then he sat back. The only reason he was in the room was that he'd wandered into the middle of their fight. "I think Daniel would probably be better at this," Fish noted.

"We enlisted his help already," Cobb countered.

Fish thought of the pages in Daniel's notebook. "He mentioned a project, but he wouldn't say what it was about . . . What's this treasure you mentioned, Melinda?"

"That's not for you to know," Cobb answered. "In fact, when you leave, you must not speak of our work here tonight."

"That includes Nate and Nora," Melinda added.

"And Daniel?"

Melinda shrugged at Cobb. "I suppose you can speak with Daniel."

Fish smiled. At least he wouldn't have to keep the secret from all his friends. "Great. So, how is the location of this treasure I'm not going to mention hidden in the coins?"

"We don't know, exactly," Melinda said.

"The coins could form a map or hide clues of some sort."

Melinda kneeled down next to him. "We noticed that these—"

"Melinda! Let the boy come to his own conclusions."

"Or we can inform him of our suspicions and move forward from there," she said, ignoring her husband's request. "Now, Fish, as I was saying, you'll notice that these twelve coins"—she pointed to the golden pile—"bear the same likeness." Melinda grouped them so each was lying flat, then flipped them so that all twelve were faceup, revealing the same small bust of a regal-looking woman—a queen, Fish guessed. "This suggests they were all minted from the same mold," Melinda added, "as they are almost exactly alike."

"Almost?" he asked.

"Yes, except for one detail." She flipped each of the coins so the queen's profile was facing down. The opposite sides were covered with images of vines and leaves wrapping around a single cursive letter. Fish slid the coins around atop the table to survey them all. A few letters were repeated on different coins. Some were unique. Did they stand for something? What did they mean?

Melinda noted his progress. "As you see, each has a single letter—"

"Can you read, Fish?"

His mother had taught Fish and his siblings the basics. She'd trained them to write, too, and he'd sharpened both skills while working for his uncle. "Yes," he replied. "Well enough."

Melinda pointed to an E on one of the coins. "So, as I was saying, each has a single letter, except for one, which has two letters, an E and an N."

Fish felt Cobb press against his other shoulder. The captain, apparently abandoning the contest with his wife, could not resist joining them. "I believe—"

The giant coughed. Cobb looked up at him. "*We* believe that if we were to arrange these coins in the proper order, there could be a message. But we have not yet discovered anything sensible."

"We think it's an anagram," Melinda added.

"The goal is to take all of the letters—R, R, D, E, Z, B, S, A, G, A, E, N, E—and rearrange them to form words," Cobb said.

"This is what Daniel has been trying to help us with," Melinda explained.

Cobb shuffled the coins until the letters, lined up, spelled BRAZENED RAGES. He slid them around a few more times, producing new arrangements of words—GREEN ZEBRAS AD, ZARBENS AGREED—but nothing that could be construed as a sensible message.

"Certainly, pirates and explorers are often brazen folk, and susceptible to rage, but 'brazened rages' blows us in no obvious direction. Naturally we assumed that 'Zarbens' in 'Zarbens agreed' would be a person, yet in our many volumes, pamphlets, and collected broadsides, neither Daniel nor the rest of us could find any record of a man—"

"Or a woman," Melinda cut in.

Impatiently, Cobb continued: "—or a woman with that name, so 'Zarbens agreed' is not our answer, either.

'Zebras' suggests we might find what we're looking for somewhere on the vast continent of Africa, but why 'green'? And why 'AD'? Unfortunately," Cobb added with a heavy sigh, "we are lost."

Fish picked up one of the gold coins and studied the woman's face. Then he examined the opposite side again and noticed something else. "A fish."

Cobb pulled on the tip of his long nose. "Focus on the letters . . . can you think of any words we've missed?"

Fish probably knew half as many words as the captain and his wife. Daniel's vocabulary stretched far beyond his own as well. If they'd been studying these coins for weeks and still hadn't discovered any hidden phrases, Fish doubted he'd be the one to find them. So he turned his attention elsewhere. "What about these?" Fish asked, pointing to the much larger pile of twenty-nine coins.

Once more Moravius coughed, as if he were trying to say something.

"Decoys," Cobb said. "Obviously mixed in with the others to mislead us."

Each of the coins in the mismatched pile was different in color and shape from the next, and in the pictures or icons on their faces, too. "So if the other coins were minted in the same place, then these might have been forged in different places, right?"

Excited, Cobb grabbed a book from his desk. The pages were thick, yellowing paper. Dozens of additional notes and folded broadsides were stuffed inside, and the whole book was wrapped tightly around with two long strips of leather. The captain untied them. He opened the book carefully, with the sort of reverence a priest reserved for the Holy Bible. A page slid halfway out; he nestled it back into place, then turned to the middle and traced his finger along one of the margins. "Nothing in here about forging them in different places. Not a word. The gold coins are the key, Fish."

When the captain looked up, he caught Fish studying the book. Suddenly secretive, Cobb closed it up, then returned it to his desk. Fish refocused on the gold coins. Still, he couldn't ignore the allure of the discarded pile. Studying two of those at once, he noticed a link between the pair. One of the coins was the size of his thumbnail, the other larger. But each bore the same icon of a bird. Nearly everything else about them was different. One featured a scene of a storm-tossed sea, the other a castle wall.

Yet they shared that single detail.

The bird had to mean something.

Melinda leaned in closely, studied what he'd uncovered.

Moravius stepped over, too. "Aha!" he said. "How simple!"

Fish jumped back from the table. The giant could speak? "Moravius!" Cobb yelled.

The giant slapped one of his enormous palms over his mouth.

"It's too late now," Melinda said. "The boy heard you. Go ahead."

"You know how he feels about this, Melinda," Cobb said. "He believes a silent, brooding giant is much more frightening than a loquacious one!"

"But he can talk?" Fish asked.

"Of course I can talk," Moravius replied.

The giant spoke with a refined accent, too.

"You may as well continue," Melinda added. "No sense pretending now that Fish knows the truth."

The giant held his breath as if he was unsure of what to do next. With one of his huge, pawlike hands, he rubbed his bearded neck and crooked nose. "This is quite a relief," Moravius began. "Although I do believe that a silent giant is more intimidating. If anyone else on board knew I was once a highly respected scholar, I'm not sure I'd have quite the same sway as I do now. I suppose I should refrain from telling Fish about my dream of cultivating orchids as well—"

"Moravius?"

"Yes, Walter?"

"We do not need a soliloquy."

"Ah, right. I apologize. Like a ship with neither sails nor tiller, caught in a current, my thoughts are afloat on—"

"Moravius!" Cobb interrupted. "We have work to do."

"Right. Yes. Of course. I am wondering, though, and maybe you could offer an opinion here, Fish, if I should shave? I've been thinking it over this past week, about how my poor skin hasn't felt a fresh breeze in years, and I believe—"

"Absolutely not," Cobb said. "The beard is essential."

Moravius appealed to Melinda. "I'm sorry, Moravius," she said. "But I think Walter is right. The beard is intimidating."

"And that?" Moravius said, pointing to the wig on Cobb's desk. "I suppose that glorified mat is essential to your image: the educated rogue?"

Cobb picked up his wig and placed it on his head. "Precisely!"

"Oh, do take it off, Walter," Melinda cut in. "It looks like a dead animal sleeping on your head."

"Or the end of a swab," Fish added.

Melinda and Moravius laughed uproariously in response. Cobb did not.

Next time, Fish would think before speaking.

"This brand is very fashionable in London!" Cobb insisted. He removed the wig and held it out. "More importantly, it serves as a reminder to the crew that I am not merely another seagoing scoundrel. I am a gentleman, a man of nobility. My father was a hero of the war, and

I was once an officer of the Royal Navy. I was educated at Cambridge!"

Melinda motioned to Moravius. "But you finished far below our friend here."

Both Moravius and Melinda resumed chuckling. Cobb's face and large ears turned purple, and Fish worried briefly that he was going to reach for his cutlass or one of the many pistols lying throughout the cabin. Instead, he traced his scar and cooled.

One of the windows rattled from a change in the breeze, and Moravius encouraged Fish to continue his study of the coins. Slowly, he sorted the rest of the pile. Each one of the twenty-nine coins was linked to at least one other through an icon like that bird. He picked out a knife, a snake, a lion, and more. These figures weren't always easy to find, as some were hidden beneath a layer of grime, but they were there.

Watching Fish work, Cobb praised every tiny discovery with enthusiasm. This was far better than being complimented on his well-scrubbed floors. When Fish glanced at Melinda, she smiled and pitched her head forward as if to say, "Don't stop now!"

The work proved fast. In just a few minutes, he had sorted the mismatched coins into nine stacks, with anywhere from two to seven coins in each: twenty-nine apparently unrelated discs sorted into piles. One stack included the coins with the figure of a snake, the next was comprised of those with a knife, then a flower, and so on. Fish arranged the stacks in a row ascending from shortest to tallest.

"What if we were wrong all along?" Moravius asked. "What if the golden coins are the decoys?"

"The letters could be random," Melinda added. "Those coins could have been tossed into the purse merely to confuse would-be treasure hunters."

"Yes," Cobb added quietly, immersed in thought, "that could be . . ."

Fish stared at the stacks. He felt a powerful urge to continue rearranging them, as if he might solve the puzzle through action alone. But he had not an inkling about how to proceed. Thankfully, he noticed that Cobb, Melinda, and Moravius were just as stumped. The captain moved back to the other side of the small room and sat on the edge of his desk, smoking his pipe, eyeing the coins with deep concentration.

Moravius remained next to Fish, bent over the table. "Perhaps the piles should be . . ." he began, then let his words trail off.

Melinda, too, muttered a half thought. "Or if we were to consider . . ."

They went on like this, alternately quiet and mumbling, for some time. Before long, the lull in the action and conversation spawned a lull in Fish's mind. The boat swayed leisurely as it sailed up and down the ocean's long, smooth waves. The excitement of his initial discovery faded, and weariness began to seep once more through his muscles and bones.

12

The Art of Not-Fighting

Fish was sleeping heavily, deep in a dream in which he was underwater, pulling potatoes out of the sandy ocean floor, when he awoke to a fierce explosion of pain in his ribs. Another one followed, in his ankle. He felt like he was being struck by a hammer. Fearing a third blow, he scampered into a crouch and held up his hands. He was back in his usual spot below. But how had he gotten there? He had a vague recollection of Moravius carrying him down. Eyes still crusted with sleep, wondering what happened to those underwater potatoes, he begged, "Stop! Please!"

"Mercy? In exchange for your blatant disregard of the rules and schedule of the ship, not to mention my very own orders?"

Scab. The stinking pirate was standing over him with Thimble at his side. He had all the rage of a bonfire in his eyes, yet red-faced, well-dressed Thimble was the one who'd been kicking him. Fish had heard that he wore wooden-toed boots. Now he'd have the bruises to prove it. "What did I do wrong?" Fish asked.

"I ordered you to clean the decks, and instead you spent the evening relaxing in the captain's quarters? Then I get word that I'm to leave you alone and not work you so hard?"

Melinda or Cobb must have said something. Now he wished they'd let him sort it out with Scab on his own. "I didn't—"

This time Scab kicked him. "Thimble, good man, how many evenings have you spent in our distinguished captain's cabin?"

The wiry tailor held out both hands as if he were ready to count the number on his fingers. Then, with mock astonishment, he answered, "Why, none!"

Fish tried to interject. "But the captain ordered—"

Scab ignored him. "An able seaman, an accomplished and experienced pirate with a noted thirst, and you have never once reclined in the captain's cabin to enjoy a bottle of his fine wine?"

"Not once!" Thimble answered. "He won't even let me mend his clothes. He has that woman do it instead, a fact that—"

"Enough!" Scab barked. "We are not down here to complain about what Cobb thinks of your needlework!

We are here to determine why it is that young Fish here has already enjoyed a privilege that is so rarely extended to the leaders of the crew. You must be a grand brand of pirate, Fish, to be invited inside after only four weeks aboard the ship."

"Ask the captain; he will—"

Thimble resumed as though Fish were not even there. "To be a great pirate, he must be a skilled fighter, too."

Scab tilted his head curiously. "I don't recall ever seeing him brandish a blade."

"Nor I."

"I must say that I should love to see this piratical prodigy in action."

"I don't fight," Fish said, his voice fired by frustration. "I don't even know how to hold a sword."

"Not a worry," Scab snapped. "You can use your fists instead."

The rogue grabbed Fish by the back of his too-large shirt and hauled him clear off the floor. Stumbling, Fish half crawled, half climbed up onto the deck as Thimble and Scab kicked him repeatedly. There was already an audience for the beating, as the men had just finished their morning exercises with Jumping Jack and were awaiting Scab's call to begin the day's work. Instead, he announced a demonstration. "For your entertainment, our newest crew member would like to display the swiftness of his fists."

Fish held up his hands, palms out, hoping to clarify

once again that he was not interested in fighting, but the crew had already begun stomping and shouting with excitement. With their appetites for action primed, there would be no calming them now. "I won't fight," Fish insisted.

"How about . . ." Scab scanned the deck and then said, "Young Nate!"

Nate stepped out of the crowd. "Sir, I would rather not—"

"Nonsense. Do you want to be a boarder or not?"

Nate stammered. He stared at Fish. They were friends now; he'd shown Fish a trick for cleaning the seats of easement in half the time. And he'd secured him a hat to keep the sun out of his eyes on bright days, too. Now the young pirate glanced back and forth between Scab and Fish. "I . . . I . . ."

"This is an order," Scab shouted. "You are a pirate, are you not?"

The question emboldened Nate. The reluctance drained from his face and posture. "I am," he said sternly.

"And you won't deny your brothers this entertainment, will you?"

"No, I will not."

Fish stiffened as he saw that Nate was eyeing him now, not Scab. They'd been given an order, and you didn't disregard orders on a pirate ship.

Nate raised his fists and began moving toward Fish.

The men whooped louder, forming a ring around the boys. Nate circled, moving slowly, as if waiting for the right moment to strike. He obviously wasn't deriving any joy from the situation, but it didn't look as if he intended to hold back, either. He rolled up his sleeves, revealing unusually large forearms for a boy his age. *If he hits me,* Fish thought, *it's going to hurt.*

At first, Fish mirrored Nate's movements, circling, raising his fists. He wasn't sure what else to do. Nate jumped closer, then backed away. The men cheered. Fish noticed Cobb, Moravius, and Melinda watching from the quarterdeck, above the captain's cabin.

"They won't save you now, boy," Scab shouted. "This is a pirate ship, in case you've forgotten!"

Another glance up at the quarterdeck revealed Scab was right. Melinda clenched her fist, as if she were urging him to strike first, and Cobb watched the scene with a slight smile.

Nora stood on a barrel, leaning against the mainmast. Daniel was nearby in the crowd.

None of them were going to intervene. That much was clear.

Scraps like this were part of the daily life on the ship.

But would they be disappointed in him if he didn't fight?

Nate lunged in and wrapped his arm around Fish's head. "What are you doing?" he whispered. "Hit me a few times, I will do the same, and it will all be over. We have to give them a show."

Nate released him; Fish looked up again at the quarter-deck. Now both Melinda and the captain gestured encouragingly, urging him to fight. Instead of spurring him to strike, though, it convinced him to stop. He was no fighter. And he never intended to become one, whether he lived among pirates or not. So he stopped, folded his hands behind his back, and proclaimed, "I refuse to fight."

Nate lowered his fists. "Fish, you can't refuse!"

Fish remained motionless with his hands behind his back.

The cheers faded. The men were confused.

Scattered boos rose up.

Noah began to sing:

> *When Nate the Great lifted up his fists*
> *And circled 'round the deck,*
> *The swab-loving Fish simply stayed in place*
> *A frozen, nervous wreck.*

"I'm not nervous!" Fish shouted over the ensuing laughs. "I said that I refuse to fight."

"But you're a pirate; you have to fight!" Nate said, pleading with him.

The Ravenous Rogues, Over and Unders, and Tea Leaves were all shouting for Fish to strike his friend.

"Hit him anyway, Nate," Scab ordered.

This time Nate didn't question the first mate.

He fired his fist like a shot from a pistol.

A very brief flash of pain erupted near Fish's left eyebrow.

Instantly, he collapsed to the deck.

FISH AWOKE NEAR THE galley, lying on a pile of sailcloth. Someone was holding a bottle of rum beneath his nose, and the fumes rushed directly to his head. His vision was blurred. He started to rub his eyes with the backs of his hands when he felt another shot of intense pain. The area above his left eyebrow was swollen from Nate's jab.

"Careful," said Daniel. "You have a nice lump there."

"I am sorry for that," said Nate. "But you should have ducked!"

Fish pushed away the bottle. He squinted; Nora was with them, too. He tried to sit up, but his head felt like it was being tossed in the waves. His friends, however, offered little sympathy.

"'I refuse to fight?'" Nora said. "What were you thinking?"

Fish clutched his stomach, which was on the edge of revolt. The only positive outcome of his eye injury was that he no longer felt the pain in his ribs from Thimble's kicks.

He took a few breaths to collect himself. No, never mind that—his entire side still ached. "I don't like fighting," he explained. "I don't think other people should fight, and I have absolutely no interest in doing so myself."

"But you're on a pirate ship!" Nora said. She pulled up one of her sleeves, revealing a hidden blade. "Even the cook fights!"

"Well," Fish said, sitting himself up, "I don't want to."

"You have to!" Nate snapped.

"Unless . . ." Daniel began.

"Unless what?" Fish asked.

"Unless we teach you how to not-fight."

Nora rolled her sleeve back down. "What?"

Daniel jumped to his feet. "Take out one of your knives and try to cut me."

"Why?"

"I'll show you."

Nora removed a small blade from her waistband and stabbed at Daniel's right shoulder. At the last instant, he rotated, and Nora only struck air. "Now the head," he said, and when Nora sliced there, he ducked. "And the stomach," he added, starting to enjoy himself. Fish thought he might jump out of the way to avoid the blade, but instead he moved only his hips, twisting and shifting. Again, Nora's strike missed its target. "You have to be fast," Daniel said, dodging the fourth, unrequested stab, "but it's something you could learn. You can use your hands, too," he added, avoiding another one of Nora's strikes by turning his shoulders and pushing her blade hand at the same time.

"Impressive," Nate said.

"I'm not going full speed," Nora noted. "How's this going to help Fish?"

"And where did you learn all that?" Nate asked.

Daniel winked at Fish. "I've been on pirate ships since I was seven years old. Sailed for two years with a crew out of Brazil. A few of the rogues on board were experts in different fighting styles. They taught me enough. Fish, you could use these tricks to duck, dodge, block, and tire your opponent out."

"Or drive them to quit from frustration," Nora said.

"Right! All of which would be better than standing there with your chin out saying, 'I refuse.' All that will earn you is an early date with the ocean floor."

The four kids were quiet for a moment. Then Nora shrugged. "It's a dangerous strategy," she said. "You'll need to be good if you're not going to use a weapon at all."

"Very good," Nate added.

"Better than me," noted Daniel. "I can try to train you, Fish."

"We all can," Nora said.

Fish considered the offer. This wouldn't count as

fighting, exactly, and he might be able to emerge from future standoffs with less painful injuries. He stood up slowly; Nate, apparently remorseful, hurried to help him to his feet. Finally, Fish looked at each of his friends in turn and, despite the dull ache above his eye, forced himself to smile. "When do we start?"

13

The Chain of Chuacar

The excitement of crossing the Atlantic faded sometime during his fifth week on the ship. He thought the thrill of being out on the open ocean, under the ceiling of bright white stars at night, would have lasted through the entire journey, but the blue water became as familiar as the farm's green fields, and the heavens were no longer any more interesting than the mist that used to settle over the cottage by dawn. His world was all wood and water now instead of fields and trees, but the unpleasant peculiarities of the ship were no longer so peculiar or unpleasant. The gruel didn't taste as awful. His stomach no longer protested the rocklike lumps of hardtack. Even his nose had trained itself to handle the new world: Scab once pressed Fish's face to one of Foot's rancid toes, and Fish inhaled without flinching. His hands adjusted, too; the raw red skin grew tough and calloused.

The not-fighting lessons with Daniel were one of the highlights of each day. At Melinda's urging, Cobb had ordered an end to Fish's night duty—which made Scab furious—so he used this time to train. As they were effectively inventing a new style of combat, they were learning as they went, but Daniel and Fish developed ways to use nearly everything on board in self-defense, including the mast, boom, tackle, barrels, and crates. They worked on using the handle of his swab, a spare line of rope, or even a belt to fend off the thrusts of a cutlass. Nate, meanwhile, considered it his role to leap or swing at Fish whenever he least expected it, and Nora occasionally hurled a hunk of hardtack at him while he ate, training him to be alert at all times. Before too long, Fish could dodge an edible projectile and easily block a sword with his swab.

As the weeks passed, more of the pirates began to recognize him as a true member of the crew. He felt like Daniel, Nora, and Nate, and not some useless newcomer. The Ravenous Rovers lectured him on the subtleties of salted meat. The Tea Leaves explained the benefits of their chosen beverage in comparison to coffee's and sang of the wonderful things their countrymen, the British, had supposedly done for his home island. The three remaining members of the Ancient Eight spoke of how to read the clouds for coming winds and demanded that he judge who among them had the worst ailments.

He especially enjoyed spending time with the Over

and Unders, who demonstrated the intricacies of different tying techniques. Knot, their leader, acted bitterly toward him at first, as Fish had caused him some embarrassment by escaping that day he saved Nate. But the pirate warmed to Fish before too long. He taught Fish how to tie and untie a range of knots, including the Slippery Noodle. Most sailors believed that only a few people in the world could untie the maze of line, but with Knot's tutelage it proved easy. Naturally, not all his interactions were friendly. Scab, Thimble, or one of their group would also mock, tease, or trip Fish whenever they had the chance.

As for the coins, and the secret he'd been asked to protect—in that assignment he'd failed. He shared what he'd learned with Daniel soon after his night in the cabin, and despite what Fish had been told, the two boys later widened their circle to include Nora and Nate. Eventually the four friends started meeting each night in secret to guess which famed treasure Cobb and Melinda sought. Daniel confided that the captain had mentioned a chain the night he was in their cabin, and Nora was convinced he'd been talking about the legendary Chain of Chuacar. One rainy evening, the boys were dining at her counter when she told them what she knew. Nora had a rare talent for storytelling. Her spin on any tale would always be two or three times longer than anyone else's rendition and far more enjoyable.

"According to the legend," she began, "Chuacar, a

mighty king, summoned one hundred of the finest crafts-men in the world to his palace following the death of his beloved wife. The king was so convinced he would never find another woman to match his lost queen that he declared the city itself to be his bride. This caused some confusion among his followers, who wondered how the king would marry an entire city. How would he talk to her? How would he look in her eyes? Did she even have eyes? If he wanted to stroke her hair, would he caress the branches of the great trees in the central square? Would people be allowed to walk through the city, or would the king complain that they were stomping all over his bride?

"One of his advisers, a young woman whose name has been lost to history, suggested that if he was going to make the city his queen, he would need to see to it that she was dressed like one. She told him it would be wise to repaint the city in bright new colors, to plant more flowers, and, most importantly, to adorn it with jewels. The adviser told him that the new queen would need earrings, which could be hung from the branches of the trees, and many large gold bracelets, which could be wrapped around the trunks. Finally, she said, the queen would need a beautiful necklace—the largest, most magnificent necklace in all the world. The king agreed, summoned his craftsmen, and ordered them to make a golden chain large enough to wrap around the whole of the city."

"The entire city?" Fish asked.

"The entire city," Nora replied.

"So what happened?" Nate asked.

"The craftsmen made the chain, but the adviser sailed off with it before the king had even seen it. Centuries passed with no word of the treasure. Then one day a lone explorer stumbled upon the chain. But it was far too large for a single man to move. He traveled on, planning to return with a crew. Years went by, and the explorer failed to gather the necessary resources. He never did return.

"Before he died, though," Nora continued, "he encoded the location of the chain in an unusual map."

"What kind of map?" Nate asked.

"I don't know," Nora said with a shrug.

Now Daniel brightened. His eyebrows rose as he removed a bundle of papers from one of his oversize pockets. Fish guessed there were ten or twelve single-page broadsides in all, each one folded over several times. Hurriedly, Daniel shuffled through them until he found the one he was looking for. He traced his finger along the page, then flipped it over and tapped a spot in the middle. "Coins," he said. "This says the map is hidden in a collection of coins." He lowered his voice to a whisper. "And they're *really* studying those coins . . ."

"What else does that say?" Nate asked, nodding to Daniel's paper.

Daniel handed it to him. "A list of the top ten undiscovered pirate treasures. The chain ranks seventh."

Nate stared oddly at the paper.

"Where do you get all those?" Fish asked.

"Every time we pull into a port, I give Melinda some coins, and she buys me every broadside and pamphlet available," Daniel said. "A pirate needs to stay informed, you know? Reading is the fastest path to expertise."

Leaning over the counter, reading the text upside down, Nora cut in. "The chain sounds too grand to be true. I think we should go for number three: the Ship with Emerald Eyes! I like the sound of that."

Nate folded up the broadside and passed it back. "Why didn't this explorer just tell people where to find it?" he asked. "Why did he make the coins?"

Daniel shrugged. "We don't even know his name."

"Legions of adventurers and treasure hunters have been searching for the treasure ever since," Nora added. "Some say the king is still looking, too—as a ghost."

Jokingly, Daniel shivered.

Fish studied his friends. Did they really want to seek this treasure? Nora and Daniel seemed excited, but Nate was clearly skeptical. And what about the rest of the crew? Scab found the very idea of a treasure hunt infuriating. A quest was a dagger to his buccaneering soul. The Ravenous Rovers? They were happy with the haul from the recent raid. Fish heard them dreaming aloud of the fine food they'd purchase when they arrived at Risden's Isle. The Ancient Eight were just happy to be alive. And Fish heard

Thimble convincing the Tea Leaves that any quest would be "a tragedy, a travesty, a terrible travail."

During one of their not-fighting sessions on deck, Fish stopped and asked Daniel what he thought. Did he want to find this chain? Or set out on more raids? His friend's response was entirely practical. Daniel admitted that he preferred a quest. Ultimately, though, his goal was to amass wealth, so if he was going to help in the search for a treasure, he wanted some assurance that it could actually be found. "Either way," Daniel concluded, "fighting will always be a part of our life, so you will need to learn to defend yourself. Are you ready?"

Fish steadied himself and prepared to not-fight.

Daniel swept his blade toward his legs. Fish jumped, pulling up his knees and feet. "Good," Daniel said. "Remember, you must exhaust your opponent, force him to quit. These pirates, they're not as quick or spry as you and I. Grog, rum, and too many years at sea have all slowed them. Disarm your opponent if possible, but if you force your foe to race around the boat, he'll give up before too long. And remember," Daniel added, "an attack could come at any time. Even here on the *Mistress*. You might be part of the same crew as these men, but they're not your friends."

Fish paused. "We're friends, though, right?"

Now Daniel stopped. He lowered his blade and his voice. "Pirates don't really have friends."

"What about the groups—Scab and his crew or the Ravenous Rovers?"

"They're not friends. They're allies."

"What's the difference?"

"Allies share the same interests, but ultimately, they live for themselves. If Scab had to choose between doubloons and Thimble's life, he'd choose the coins. Same with the Ancient Eight and the Ravenous Rovers. Even Cobb would probably ditch Melinda and Moravius for the right amount."

"That's not true!"

"What do you know?" Daniel snapped. "You've been on the ship for a few weeks and you already know the captain better than the rest of us?"

"Well . . ." Fish had seen and sensed a very real and deep bond between the giant, Cobb, and Melinda. The suggestion that the captain, too, was a coin-crazed rascal who valued treasure above love or friendship—it simply was not true. And Daniel needed to know that. "The night I was in the cabin, they didn't seem like mere allies."

"You say that like it's a bad word."

"The way you describe it, I think it is. To value yourself and money above all else? That's not what I saw. Not what I heard. They were more like a family."

Daniel held out his cutlass, a wordless warning that their lessons were to resume. He jabbed in at half speed, and Fish still moved aside too late.

"Try again. And remember: Know where you are on the boat."

Once again, Daniel's thrust was successful. He stopped short of injuring his friend, but Fish felt the pressure of the blade against his chest. He squeezed his eyes closed, furious with himself.

Daniel stopped. "You're thinking too hard. It slows you down if you think and plan before you act. You don't think when you walk, do you?"

"No."

"When you swim?"

"No."

"Right! And in a fight, or a not-fight, you can't think. You have to react."

As he pronounced the last word, Daniel jumped forward, thrusting his cutlass at full speed. Fish felt himself move to the side, watched his hands lash out, grab the hilt, and pull the sword forward, jamming it into the mast.

Daniel laughed. "See? React! Don't think."

The handle of the weapon swung back and forth. Fish wished they could keep the cutlass there. The sight of it filled him with pride. But Daniel yanked out his sword, and the two boys sat down and gazed up at the stars.

"Hey, Daniel?" Fish asked.

"Yes?"

"You and me. Are we allies, at least?"

"No, Fish," he replied, "we're not allies."

An uncomfortable silence followed. Fish wished he could retract the question.

Then Daniel surprised him. "We're friends, and I'll prove it to you."

Fish didn't need proof; the unexpected statement was more than enough. He had a real, actual, true friend. He was beyond excited. He felt taller than Moravius himself. "I trust you, Daniel. You don't need to—"

"And I'm going to place my trust in you, too, as a friend."

Daniel scurried under the steps leading up to the quarterdeck. "Here," he said, pointing to a small square panel in the wooden deck, in the darkness below the steps. "Open that."

Fish, on his knees in the small space, removed the panel.

"Go ahead, reach in," Daniel said.

His fingers closed around a cloth purse harboring something large and metallic. He picked it up, then moved into a beam of blue-gray moonlight sneaking through the space between two steps. The purse was heavily embroidered and studded with small stones. He pulled out a silver key inlaid with gems matching those on the purse. "A key?"

"Not so loud!" Daniel whispered, checking to see whether anyone had heard. "Of course it's a key!"

"To what?"

"To my sea chest. Most pirates carry their keys around

121

their necks. If you choose to hide it, you don't tell any-one . . . unless you're lucky enough to have a friend."

Now Fish felt as tall as the ship's mast. He was soaring. Carefully, he slipped the key back into the purse, admiring the embroidery, the tiny gems sparkling in the moon-light. The purse was a treasure in and of itself. "Thank you, Daniel. I've never really had a friend . . . and your friendship . . ."

He couldn't think of what to say or how to say it; he stared at the purse as Daniel returned it to its hiding place.

Suddenly, a spark ignited in his mind.

The purse.

The coins.

Reginald Swift!

Fish leaped to his feet. "That's it! That's the secret!"

His friend was understandably confused. "What's the secret?" Daniel asked.

Before Fish could answer, Scab roared, "Minnow!" The pirate was stomping toward them from the other side of the ship. "What are you two worthless deckhands conspiring about?"

Fish readied himself for a swing of Scab's fist, or maybe a hastily thrown mug.

Daniel addressed him calmly. "Nothing, sir."

"Good," Scab growled. His mouth stretched into a vile smile. "There's a seat of easement on the port side newly in need of your affection, Fish."

Daniel nodded to Fish, wordlessly indicating that they'd discuss matters later.

Meanwhile, Fish grabbed his swab and followed Scab's orders. Despite the disgusting nature of the assignment, he couldn't help smiling. The work was undeniably repulsive, yet his mood was bright, as there was a chance he'd just unlocked the secret to finding the treasure.

14

Hidden Key

Later, when the dreadful work was done, and Scab had gone below, Fish hurried into the captain's cabin. Cobb, Melinda, and Moravius were sitting together around the table, the coins stacked before them. As he burst into the room, they looked up, more shocked than outraged. He slammed the door shut. "The purse!" Fish blurted. "Where is it?"

"What purse?" Cobb asked.

"The one that held the coins. Do you have it?"

Cobb looked at Melinda, who turned to Moravius, who relayed the exchange back to the captain.

"We need to find it! I think it will help us make sense of the coins."

Cobb jumped to his feet, knocking into the table on his way up. "Scour the cabin!"

"The scouring would be easier if the two of you kept the place clean," Moravius said.

"Not now! Lift your gargantuan frame out of that chair and help us."

The giant discovered the purse under several stacks of leather-bound journals and books written in languages Fish did not recognize. Moravius tossed it to him, and Fish set to work as he explained the source of his theory.

"When I met the Swifts on the dock," he said, "they mentioned that the purse itself was as important as the coins."

Now, emptied of its contents and pressed flat, the purse was not much larger than one of his hands. Dark brown and aged, it had been made from a single piece of leather doubled over and sewn up along the seams. There was a metal clasp attached near the top to close it tight.

Fish examined every fiber, every wrinkle. He studied the clasp, the seams running up along each side of the purse. Nothing. But what had he expected? Instructions? That would've been too simple. He turned the purse inside out.

"There!" Cobb yelled.

"How simple," Moravius muttered.

Melinda excitedly wrapped Fish in her thick arms.

There were several circular imprints burned into the leather, each with a small icon in the center. The flower, the bird, the knife—they were all there. The icons on the twenty-nine coins matched the ones on the purse. Hands shaking with anticipation, Fish laid the purse on the table and flattened it out. There were six circles lined up in a row on one side; he flipped it over and counted another six. A single line ran below them, or above, depending on which way he held the purse. If he could tear open the seams along either side, he'd have a single strip of leather with those imprints in a single row. But he lacked the strength to pull it apart. This purse had remained intact through years of wear and travel; it wasn't going to succumb to his small hands. When Moravius understood what he was trying to do, the giant tore it open with ease.

Now Fish had before him a large band of leather. The two sets of six circles were arranged in a straight line. A simple dash separated them in the middle, where the bottom of the purse had been folded. Another, longer line stretched below the circles. He rotated it so that this line was on top, then switched back.

"It must be a series," Melinda decided. "In which case that line should probably be on the bottom. That way, we know which circle is meant to be first."

The first circle featured an icon of a serpent, the second a bird. In the middle of the third, there was an image of a tree, in the fourth a knife, in the fifth a lion, then a flower, a horse, a boat, and, in the ninth position, a crown. Finally, in the last three circles, one of the elements was repeated.

Each of them contained a simple picture of a flower, just like the sixth.

Two of the coins bore the icon of the serpent. Fish moved this short stack into that first circle. In the next circle there was a bird, so he picked up the corresponding stack and moved that pair into position.

Next, he looked for the coins bearing the image of the tree and placed another stack of two into the third circle. Three coins filled the fourth circle, all of them with the symbol of a knife. Another three coins matched the lion in the fifth position. Four fit with the flower in the sixth spot. Melinda squeezed his shoulder with encouragement. He slid seven coins into the seventh circle, three into the eighth, and another stack of three into the ninth.

At the tenth position, Fish stopped and stared. No coins remained. Yet each of the last three circles shared the same icon as the sixth: the flower. Had he erred somehow? Yes! He'd placed that stack of four coins into a single circle when he should have distributed them evenly among all four—one flower coin in each of the corresponding circles.

He followed through, and then he was finished. But with what?

"Brilliant!" Moravius muttered.

"What's brilliant?" Cobb asked.

"Don't you see? Six here, six there?"

The captain did not see. Neither did Melinda. And Fish

remained utterly perplexed. Moravius knelt next to Fish at the edge of the desk and began counting the coins in each stack. "Two, two, two, three, three, one. Then seven, three, three, one, one, one."

Cobb's face was blank. "And?"

"If it's a verse from Homer, you may as well tell us," Melinda said with a sigh.

"No!" Moravius said. "Latitude and longitude! Two-two, then two-three, and then three-one. Then seven-three, three-one, one-one."

Cobb's eyes opened wide. "Of course! Twenty-two hours, twenty-three minutes, thirty-one seconds by seventy-three hours, thirty-one minutes, eleven seconds."

Fish thought he'd heard the terms "latitude" and "longitude" before—he remembered Daniel mentioning them. But he couldn't recall what they meant. "I don't understand. Is that a time?"

"No," Melinda explained. "It's more of an address. Think of the Earth as being crisscrossed with these lines, the way a city is a grid of streets. Given a precise line of latitude and a corresponding line of longitude, we can pinpoint any spot on the globe."

Cobb grabbed Fish by the shoulders with unexpected force. "Fish, you may very well have discovered the location that has eluded countless treasure hunters!"

"One problem," Moravius said. He was hunched over a

map of the world. "Seventy-three longitude is on the other side of the Earth."

A noise just outside the cabin pulled away their attention. An alarmed Cobb glanced at Moravius. The giant stepped quietly and quickly to the door, then thrust it open. Yet no one was there. Moravius ducked and moved out onto the deck, inspecting the area. Fish glanced through the doorway. A small bucket lay overturned nearby—it could have fallen from the quarterdeck. Moravius held it up for Cobb to see, shrugged, and stepped back inside.

The captain moved over to the line of coins and shifted his wig. Fish watched his brow tighten. Cobb pushed his fist against his forehead, just above his long nose. And then he smiled.

"What is it?" Moravius asked.

Cobb was glowing. "Do you mean you don't know? But it is so apparent. A simple—"

"Cease gloating, Walter," Melinda interjected.

Cobb pointed to the dash imprinted in the leather. "Not seventy-three. Negative seventy-three!"

"What does that mean?" Fish interrupted.

"It means we're close," Melinda whispered. "We're actually close."

Now Fish glanced at the pile of gold coins—the ones with the letters. "What about those?"

"A final clue, perhaps?" Moravius suggested.

"Or maybe they're decoys after all," Melinda noted.

"Never mind them," Cobb declared. "We have our location. We'll sail north from Risden's Isle. From there I expect a week's sail at most."

"A week's sail to where?" Fish asked.

"To the Chain of Chuacar!"

15

Cobb's Quest

As Fish barraged them with questions about the chain, Cobb asked him to be patient, then grabbed a package from his desk and invited him up to the quarterdeck. Daniel was still down below, and he didn't see Nate or Nora, either, but he was going to tell his friends everything at the first chance. There would be no more secrets between them.

The wind was steady but quiet that night, and the *Scurvy Mistress* moved slowly through the waves. A bright half-moon shone in a cloudless sky, and for the first few minutes, the captain simply watched the water, smoking his pipe. There were a million questions Fish wanted to ask, but Uncle Gerry had taught him not to interrupt a man while he's smoking. Finally, Cobb spoke. "Melinda, Moravius, and I have been searching for the Chain of Chuacar for more than ten years. Almost as long as you've been alive. The chain takes up more pages in my book than any other treasure."

"Your book?"

Cobb lowered his voice and leaned in. "My collected research notes on the world's greatest treasures. I saw you eyeing it that first night in the cabin. Many a rogue would give their firstborn for that book. Then again, many pirates would sacrifice their children for much less, so maybe that's not a good example."

Briefly, Fish wondered what other treasures were discussed inside those leather-bound pages. Then he thought of Reidy Merchants. "How did my uncle become involved?"

Cobb puffed out a mouthful of smoke. "Any merchant in any port town conducts business with pirates on occasion. Bakers sell us their bread; brewers, their beer. This does not make them brigands. Nevertheless, Reidy Merchants is a known agent in our world."

"The pirate world?"

"The world of treasure hunting in particular. We are not the only ship of our kind, as I'm sure you know, and we are not the only people in search of the chain, either. There are other pirates, like ourselves, and landed folk, too, who hire adventurers to search out these treasures for them."

"Reginald Swift and his mother," Fish guessed.

"Correct. His mother, who insists on calling herself Lady Swift, is a very successful and utterly ruthless treasure hunter. Do not let her grandmotherly appearance deceive you. That woman is as cunning as a viper and as sharp as any sword. She hired your uncle to organize a crew to retrieve the coins. Thankfully, one member of that crew was willing to share this information with us, for a price, so we knew when and where your uncle was due to pass along the coins. Lady Swift was on her way to collect them when—"

"Nate swiped them from me," Fish said.

Cobb put a hand on his shoulder. "That was not your fault," he said. "If Nate hadn't succeeded, we would have found another way to secure them. Besides, Lady Swift is no longer any concern of ours," he added with a smile. "The only thing between us and the chain is open water."

The captain smiled down at him, then resumed smoking as Fish tried to make sense of all he'd heard. He still had questions. "From the stories I heard, only one man knew the location of the chain."

"An English explorer and adventurer. Wentworth Collins."

"I thought his name was lost to history?"

"Not to me," Cobb said with a smile.

Fish thought of the question Nate had asked when they were looking at Daniel's broadside. "Why would Collins go to the trouble of making such complex coins? Why wouldn't he just tell someone where to find the chain?"

"Treasure hunters are a strange and inexplicable group, Fish! We spend years, decades, entire lives, searching for glorious, legendary riches that may not exist. We will never know how Collins himself discovered the chain, but I suspect that he struggled mightily in his quest and found the idea of someone else uncovering that treasure without an equally significant struggle too deplorable to bear. Leaving the rest of us something so simple as a map would have been an insult! The coins are truly the work of a man obsessed. A man more interested in the search for treasure than treasure itself."

"But what if it's all a trick?"

The captain sucked in on his pipe and shrugged. "Then we will be in grave danger. Myself especially."

"Why you?"

"If our quest fails, I imagine Scab will rally enough souls on this ship to force me to walk the plank."

"I could teach you how to swim—"

The captain laughed, choking on smoke. When he recovered, he patted Fish on the back. "Maybe one day, Fish, but we don't need to worry ourselves now. We will find the chain." After another long draw on his pipe, Cobb took out the package he'd removed from his desk. "I have something for you," he said.

Wrapped in the cloth, Fish found a strange pair of eyeglasses: two large, round pieces of glass framed in wood, then cushioned with waxed leather. Cloth ties dangled off each side. "Thank you, sir . . . but what are they?"

"They're swimming glasses! For Fish the pirate."

The captain placed the glass circles over Fish's eyes and tied the straps behind his head to create a tight seal. The wooden rims and bridge held the glass away from his eyes, and the leather cushioned the wood so it didn't press too hard into his skin.

"Wear them underwater. They must be tight, or water will leak in. I've had them for a long, long time but never found much use for them. Melinda and I decided that if you are so drawn to the water, you might as well see what the world looks like down there."

Fish didn't know what to say. Back home, the only presents he'd ever received, besides the carving from Roisin, were particularly well-shaped potatoes or patches of cloth to cover new holes in his pants. He managed to say "thank you" a few times, then stood with the goggles still on his face, gazing out at the dark water. He wanted to dive in right then and there.

Cobb started chuckling. "You can take them off now, Fish. You'll have plenty of opportunities to test them where we're going."

Embarrassed, Fish coughed and stared out again at the open water.

Bright stars filled the entire sky, straight down to the horizon.

"Fish, I believe there's a reason you came to our ship," Cobb said. "I believe you have great potential."

"Potential?"

"You could make a great treasure hunter one day. Perhaps even a captain."

In Fish's head a vision appeared: He was standing on the bridge of the *Scurvy Mistress*, much older, with a pipe in his hand and a huge scar across his forehead. An odd scene, and not altogether believable. "A pirate captain?"

"That is for you to decide. Each of us must determine our place in the world on our own."

"I'm not sure I could ever control a group like this," Fish said.

"No one can," Cobb answered, "but I've watched you with them, Fish. They like you. Most of them, anyway, and that is essential. A great captain doesn't control his men. He inspires loyalty."

"I'm not certain Scab would be loyal to me."

Cobb removed his knife, ran the blade carefully down his jaw as if it were a shaving razor. The metal gleamed in the moonlight. "Since the day seven years ago when we captured his ship, I have been watching Scab's every move, knowing full well that he could start a mutiny at any time."

"Then why keep him on? Why make him your second-in-command?"

"Because he's one of the most skilled swordsmen I've ever seen. He is absolutely fearless, and a brilliant sailor; he could handle this ship all alone if need be. Sailing across the world, dodging the naval ships of the world's greatest nations, is no easy task, Fish. Eluding capture requires men like Scab. Furthermore, I would rather have him on board the *Scurvy Mistress* as part of my crew, where I can watch him, than sailing his own sloop. If he were to leave, he'd probably raid us within a matter of weeks.

"You see, Fish, Scab is a different breed from Moravius, Melinda, and me. There are two sides to the pirate business. One involves plundering ships."

"The raids," Fish said.

"Right. The true raider, like Scab, is only interested in capturing prizes, and that's how most pirates measure success. But when you conduct raids, you make enemies. Powerful ones! This brand of pirate can never stop and think. He needs to keep moving. He needs to keep capturing prizes."

"I could see Scab enjoying that life, though."

"Exactly! If Scab had his way, we'd capture every ship we saw."

"What about you?"

"I'm a seeker, Fish. I'll take a prize now and then, to keep the crew satisfied and the ship stocked, but I'd prefer we spend our efforts hunting down the great treasures that the Scabs of the world are too restless to pursue."

Cobb gazed out at the water. A wide beam of blue-white moonlight played on the surface, like a path leading straight to the edge of the earth. The captain yawned and announced that it was time for sleep.

"Captain?" Fish said.

"Yes?"

"I think I'm a seeker, too."

Cobb smiled. "Yes, Fish. I think you are."

16

Festering Scab

Two weeks had passed since Fish's conversation with Cobb. Two weeks of deck swabbing, not-fighting, learning about knots, discussing the optimal degree of saltiness in salami, and, whenever possible, sleeping. The night of his meeting with Cobb, Fish confided in Daniel, telling him everything he'd learned. The next morning, the pair of them told Nora and Nate. They all swore one another to secrecy. Daniel was excited but confused, too. He refused to believe the letters on the gold coins were merely a distraction.

Meanwhile, the ship sailed on. Fish had been on the *Scurvy Mistress* just two months, but he couldn't remember what it felt like to stand on solid, unwavering ground. He hadn't done any swimming, either, but he kept Cobb's gift tied to his waist so he'd be ready to use the swimming glasses at his first chance.

Fish was scrubbing the floor beside the galley one morning when the men on deck began cheering and yelling. Nora raced out, green eyes bright with energy. She brushed her hands on her dress, which was, given its tattered condition and abundant stains, really just one large apron. "Quick!" she said. "I think we've spotted land!"

The two friends rushed up to the deck and hurried to the edge of the ship with the rest of the crew. The land was little more than a lump on the horizon. Fish couldn't discern many details, but the water! The water was absolutely beautiful. In only a day, the color had changed from dark green to crystal-clear blue. The sun was stronger, too. Altogether, it felt like another world.

Excitedly, Daniel called them up to the bow. Three porpoises—Nora and Daniel had to tell Fish what they were, since he'd never seen anything like them—were diving in and out of the water, playing in front of the ship as it cut through the small waves. Fish found himself smiling wider than he had in months. The long journey, the terrible food, the endless days spent in the stinking, filthy quarters below—it had all been worthwhile.

Noah and a group began singing:

Land ho!
Land ho!
Where the trees and flowers grow
And the ocean's waves don't flow,

Land ho!
Land ho!

The mood changed after this first sighting of solid ground. The pirates worked and sang with added vigor. Even their fights were joyful. At one point, Knot punched Sammy the Stomach in the jaw, and the voracious gunner began laughing. At first, Fish assumed it was the prospect of planting their feet on dry earth that had turned the crew delirious, or the idea of sleeping on a mat that didn't roll and swing like a hammock, but Daniel explained that it wasn't land in general, but a particular location. They were up top at the time, with Nora and Nate and much of the crew. A few days had passed since the first sighting of land, and they were now between islands, the horizon blank before them.

"It's called Risden's Isle, and it's a pirate paradise," Daniel said. "The harbor is guarded by six big guns mounted high on the cliffs to keep out unwanted visitors. There are four inns, five pubs, and the best food you'll ever eat. The sharpest knives, the most reliable pistols, anything you want you'll find on Risden's Isle."

"Thimble always drinks the place dry of wine, then buys all the linens and silks they have so he can make his fancy shirts and scarves," Nate said.

"Sammy the Stomach buys more sausage than you could eat in a year," Nora said.

"The Salty Scabbard," Nate said, "has perfectly cooked crabs."

Nora agreed, then added, "The stew at the Rusty Anchor is wonderfully spicy."

"And you can't leave without enjoying a bite at Dancing Dan's," Nate urged.

"What about you, Daniel? Any favorite spots on the island?" Fish asked.

After a pause, Daniel sighed and answered, "I've never been. I haven't been off the ship in two years. The last time I put my feet on land, there was a tempest in my stomach. The rolling of a ship at sea is my stability; without it I become violently ill. Some people get seasick, I suffer from land-sickness. I'm not the only one, though. You'll rarely see Bat or Owl ashore. It's a common affliction. But you'll bring me back a few items, won't you? I'll give you a list."

"Of course I will," Fish answered.

The *Scurvy Mistress* sailed for three more long days before Daniel, perched atop the mast early one morning and staring toward a horizon blurred by fog, shouted, "Risden's Isle ahead!"

Holding on to his swab, Fish rushed to the side of the ship with the other men, who were ready to dance with glee. Noah broke into song:

Where the trees are bright and green
And the food so fine and clean,

I'll rest there for a good long while,
Spend my gold on Risden's Isle.

Fish heard the men say they were at least an hour away. He'd be expected to resume his work down below, so he started that way when a hand clamped down on his shoulder. Without thinking he reacted, dropping to a crouch and turning his shoulders. The lessons with Daniel were working! He'd moved with the person who tried to grab him, eluding the man's grasp. And he'd done it without thinking. Yet the owner of the hand was hardly ready to issue congratulatory remarks. Scab growled. "Where are you going?"

"To swab belowdecks," Fish answered.

"Now is not the time for swabbing!" Scab said, the metallic hoops stuck through his face shining in the sunlight. "Risden's isn't all food and fun. An island full of pirates means an island full of fighting. We don't want you to shame us all if you can't hold your own. So let's see if you're ready, Fish."

"May I scrap with the runt?" Thimble asked, placing his hand on the hilt of his cutlass.

"No," Scab answered. "Allow me."

The first mate raised his fists.

"No, thank you," Fish said, backing away, "this will hardly be necessary."

Scab's thick fist, large enough for a man twice his size, and with countless tarnished rings jammed between the knuckles, flashed forward. Again, without thinking, Fish ducked. The punch merely grazed his ear. Scab, snarling, his face knotted with frustration behind his ragged beard, raised his fists once more. Those rings! They'd leave dents in Fish's forehead.

Scab swung from another angle. Fish dodged and stepped away. He had to keep talking, try to reason with him. "Really, I don't think it's necessary. You are obviously a far more skilled fighter and—"

"You do not decide what is and is not good for you!" Scab shouted. "Any ship is only as strong as its weakest rib, and you, boy, are the weakest rib!"

Quickly, Fish studied his surroundings. *Find where you're comfortable.* That's what Daniel had said. Unfortunately, he still had not figured that out. The stairs to the quarterdeck were back over his right shoulder. The mast was a few paces ahead. Three barrels stood to his left. Where was he comfortable? Nowhere.

"What if I promise to avoid all conflicts on shore?" he suggested. Scab punched again and missed. "Really," Fish reasoned, moving toward the barrels, "I am rather good at avoiding conflict."

Fish's response produced a few eruptions of laughter. He glanced around; more members of the crew were walking over to watch. Nate, Daniel, and Nora were among them, but he knew they could not intervene. This would be Fish's fight to win or lose.

No—his fight to avoid.

Slowly, Scab pulled his cutlass from his belt. "Where's your weapon?"

"I don't have one," Fish said, "and I don't need one."

They continued to circle each other. Scab would not be talked down. There were too many people watching now, and he wouldn't stand to be embarrassed.

"I don't see why you need a blade, either. I'm merely a boy."

"Cut the little rat!" someone yelled.

Several other men responded in Fish's favor.

"Pick that scab, Fish!"

"Drain that pile of pus!"

These shouts seemed to weaken Scab's resolve.

The pirate began to sheathe his weapon.

Fish felt his tense legs relax. He'd done it. He'd stopped the fight without a punch! Fish looked to Daniel, his friend and teacher, for approval. But urgency flared in his friend's eyes. Scab sneered, revealing his cracked brown teeth. Suddenly his cutlass flew out. Fish was too slow to react. Scab pinned him with one hand up against a barrel and, with the other, pressed the blade to his throat. The pirate's hot, rancid breath blew against his face. After all those lessons with Daniel, all those nights of not-fighting, Fish had failed. The men were booing. Daniel, Nate, Nora, and even Cobb would all be disappointed in him. Scab was right. He was the weakest rib.

The pirate sheathed his blade and grabbed Fish by the hair, as if he were pulling a clump of weeds out of a field. Fish gritted his teeth, closed his eyes, and tried to yank Scab's hand away, but there was no unleashing that grip. Fish stumbled, struggling as the pirate pulled him across the deck, every misstep causing Scab to pull harder. The pain was like nothing he'd ever experienced.

At the railing, Scab let go of his hair and grabbed him by the shirt, pulling him close so they were face-to-face. Fish didn't even try to struggle. Scab's breath burned in his nose, coated the inside of his mouth. Fish tried to look away, to avoid the man's black eyes, bright red scars, and brown, half-wrecked teeth.

"You're a fish, are you?" Scab whispered menacingly. "Well, then, go back to where you belong."

And the pirate hoisted him over the side and into the water.

17

Risden's Isle

line had been tossed into the sea. Fish grabbed hold and was dragged along behind the ship. His friends were at the starboard rail. Nate was securing the rope. He risked Scab's wrath with that alone, and Fish guessed Nate wouldn't dare pulling him aboard as well. Yet he wasn't ready to return anyway. Fish was too ashamed to rejoin the crew.

He let the sea wash over him, draining the sickening intensity of the fight from his body. The water was neither hot nor cold; it felt perfectly matched to his skin. He felt as if he were part of it. And the sea here was so clear! The water was far deeper than the deepest part of Outhouse Lake, and yet, even from above, at the wavy surface, he could see straight to the ocean floor. Remembering Cobb's gift, he reached down to his waist, untied the swimming glasses, and with the line wrapped around one arm, fastened them around his eyes. A deep breath, then another, and he dropped down below the surface. The line dragged him through a multicolored underwater world full of purple fernlike waving plants, giant yellow rocks covered with small grooves and channels, fish of all shapes and colors and sizes. Schools of brightly striped minnows darted and dodged in unison, as if they were all obeying the inaudible orders of some underwater captain. Only when it felt like Moravius was standing on his chest did Fish remember that he was not, in fact, one of these silvery minnows, but a kid who needed air to live. He kicked back up to the surface, sucked in a few restorative breaths, and dove down once more.

Fish had been dragging behind the ship for an hour when the *Scurvy Mistress* anchored in Risden's Isle's heavily guarded harbor. The crew rowed for shore in the single launch, six men per trip. Thimble and Sammy the Stomach fought their way into the first boat, driven by extreme thirst and unmatched hunger, respectively. Fish himself swam and dove around the harbor for a while before crawling up onto the flour-like white sand. Exhausted, he stumbled from the water's edge to a grove of odd trees with tall, skinny, branchless trunks that reached up to a thin canopy of leaves. He stretched his shirt out to dry in the sun, lay down on the shady sand, and fell into a heavy and dreamless sleep.

Evening had arrived when Fish awoke. His stomach

was growling. What had Nora said was her favorite place? The Salty Scabbard? No, that was Nate's spot. The Rusty Anchor? Yes, that's where he'd go first. Fish eased to his feet and understood instantly why Daniel preferred to stay aboard. His head spun. His stomach switched from ravenous to queasy. The solid ground was now as alien to him as the rocking deck of the ship had been when they first set sail.

A dirt path led up and out of the harbor. He shook the sand off his dry, salt-encrusted shirt and started walking. Luckily, his brief spell of land-sickness soon faded. At the top of the hill, the path opened into a large town square crowded with loud, dirty, ragged pirates. The air was packed with the smells of sizzling charred meats, burning spices, baking breads, the sweetness of many-flavored soups and stews. The three Ancient Eight were sitting with their arms around one another, gripping great silver mugs overflowing with grog and singing to the rising moon. A fourth pirate was slumped beside them, snoring heavily.

The buildings were belching songs and shouts and cheers through wide-open windows and doors. Fish absorbed all the sights, sounds, and smells with wonder. He spotted the Salty Scabbard to his right and Dancing Dan's nearby. The rogues inside the latter were singing and drinking, carousing and eating, and, of course, fighting. There were more women in the town than he expected, including an especially fierce, all-female crew of pirates.

One of the Ravenous Rogues made the mistake of offending one of these women, and she belted him so hard in the stomach that he chose to crawl to safety rather than stand and fight back.

A horde burst from a doorway behind him, rushing out like sheep loosed from a pen. Fish spotted Noah in the throng, pencil and nails still stuck behind his ears. He didn't see the captain, Melinda, or Moravius, and guessed they were dining inside one of the pubs. When he eyed Nate and Nora crossing the square, though, he tried to hide, still ashamed by his performance on the *Scurvy Mistress*. Yet his friends quickly spotted him and rushed to his side. Both reassured him.

"You did fine," Nate said. "Next time you'll not-fight him to sleep."

The relief was tremendous; he couldn't hide his smile. "I'm hoping there isn't a next time," Fish replied.

"Let's turn to more important matters. Where should we eat?" Nora asked.

"How about that place?" Fish asked, pointing to the least threatening pub.

"Great!" Nora answered. "That's the Rusty Anchor. They have gorgeous beef, roasted on a spit with a garden's worth of herbs."

The origin of the pub's name was evident immediately after they walked inside. In the middle of the room was a massive, rusted anchor, lying there as if cut loose from some sky-going ship. After settling into a corner table, they ordered stew, roasted pig, and servings of beef. Fish set in right away when the plates arrived. The beef was blackened on the outside, encrusted with charred herbs, emanating smells he could not describe, and moist in the center. He devoured the first bite, then several more, before noticing that Nora and Nate were staring. "What?"

"It's as if you haven't eaten in weeks."

That was exactly how he felt, but of course he couldn't say this aloud. "No, it's not that—"

"Stop," Nora said. "I won't be offended."

The roasted pig was his favorite. On special occasions, they enjoyed pork on the farm, but it had never tasted like this, so sweet and fall-apart delicious. Two mouthfuls into his first plate, he ordered a second, and they sat sharing stories and dreams. Nora spoke of her longing to get out from behind that galley counter and earn a higher rank. Nate hoped aloud that he'd be a great captain one day.

"You will," Nora said. "I know it."

Nate blushed at the comment, then quickly stood up from the table to conceal his embarrassment. "Daniel's waiting. We should get back. I'll settle our account."

"No, you don't have to—" Nora began.

"Please, allow me," Nate said.

Fish began to object, too, then stopped and laughed.

"What is it?" Nora asked.

"I ordered two plates of pork, two servings of beef, and I don't know how many glasses of milk."

"And?"

"And I don't have a single coin to my name."

His two friends laughed. "It's on us," Nate said with a smile.

They ordered for Daniel, too, and brought him a massive dinner that night. The next three days were packed with exhausting work. From first light until nearly dusk, with only an hour's rest at noon, Fish was in the water, scraping the underwater portion of the hull free of barnacles and sea greenery. He'd forgotten this was one of the tasks Cobb had mentioned when he was assessing whether Fish would be a suitable member of the crew. All the weeds and crustaceans that had accumulated over a year of neglect had begun to slow the ship. Without them, the hull would cut more smoothly and swiftly through the seas. Fish understood the value of the work, but this did not lessen the pain. His hands and fingers cramped, the muscles pulling them into unnatural alignments. His lungs ached from holding his breath. And he was probably going to have permanent depressions around his eyes from wearing his swimming glasses all day.

While he was in the water, Daniel and Nate worked on the ship, filling the seams with oakum and pitch to prevent leaks, all under Noah's direction. Nora was busily restocking. With Foot and a few of his assistants, she purchased new supplies, including barrels of flour and drink.

The days were long, but the evenings were delightful. After finishing his work, Fish would swim ashore and eat with Nate and Nora at the Rusty Anchor. The other pubs were too rough and rowdy, and the food, Nora said, was no better. Afterward, they'd grab an extra dinner for Daniel, signal for someone from the *Scurvy Mistress* to retrieve them, then sit on the deck together, telling stories and talking piracy. Daniel was a true historian of pirate culture. He knew all there was to know about the great raiders and treasure hunters, and quite a bit about the obscure ones, too. Before long, his friends knew Fish's entire history as well: the farm, Outhouse Lake, his brothers and sisters, his gruff father and stern, strong mother, and his mysterious uncle Gerry. It felt good to tell them. It made him feel less alone.

Most of the pirates slept ashore, so on these nights, the four friends felt like lords of the ship, kings and queen of the sea. With the moon and stars bright in the night sky, the water flat and calm, the leaves of the onshore trees dancing in the light breeze, Fish could've sworn he'd entered paradise.

ON THE MORNING OF the fourth day, Fish dove into the harbor and found that the hull was perfectly clean.

Any more attention from his scraping blade and he'd be scratching off cedar. Cobb happened to be on board when he finished.

"And only three days!" he said when Fish gave his report. "I suppose it hasn't been that long since our last cleaning, but that's impressive work, Fish. Very impressive. The men are fortified and refreshed, so I suspect we'll be embarking on our quest for the treasure very soon. Take today to enjoy the island."

A week earlier, his chosen form of leisure would have been firmly aquatic, but after spending the majority of his last three days in the water, he wanted to feel the earth beneath his feet. Nora had said the walk to the top of the island's highest point was rewarding, so he proposed a hike to his friends.

"A marvelous idea," Nora replied.

"I'll bring a bow," Nate added. "I've heard there's prized game in the hills."

"What about you?" Fish asked Daniel. "You don't want to try?"

His land-averse friend shook his head.

Nate bought a small bow and a quiver of arrows from Dolphin Dry Goods, the island's general store. Nora, whose normally pale skin had begun to tan from a few days out in the sun, bought herself a hat, and the three of them marched off into the woods. Nate was quiet and vigilant, as if a great lion could emerge at any second. He was clearly trying to impress Nora, but Fish could see she needed no convincing. The way she watched him, admiring his careful eye, made it obvious their attraction was mutual.

The trees became shorter and thicker as they climbed, their leaves boasting a deeper shade of green. It had rained the night before, and although the town had since dried, everything here remained wet. Eventually, they came to a clearing three-quarters of the way up the hill and stopped to view the vast turquoise sea flattened out behind them.

This should have been an uplifting view.

Even triumphant.

Yet Fish's gaze was drawn immediately to a well-traveled sloop with bright white sails nearing the entrance to the harbor. He had seen that ship before, first in the harbor back in Ireland, then after the raid of the *Mary*.

"She's familiar," Fish said.

"Yes," Nate answered, his voice solemn. "Yes, she is."

"We need to tell the captain," Nora declared.

Fish started to agree, but she was already hurrying down the hill.

18

Swimming Spy

In the town square, they spotted Noah first, outside the Salty Scabbard, and told him what they'd seen. Fish asked if he'd seen the captain. They needed to tell him, Nora added. Noah scratched his dark beard. He knew the make and build of ships better than anyone and pressed them with a few extra questions about the curve of the hull. After pondering their responses for a moment, he replied, "That is indeed a strangincidence."

"A what?"

Impatiently, Nora exhaled. "A strange coincidence," she explained. "Clever, Noah. But tell us, where is Cobb?"

A familiar growl interrupted their exchange. "Why do you need Cobb?" A metal mug in one hand, the other resting on the hilt of his cutlass, Scab stood watching them. Fish didn't even want to look at the first mate. Not after their fight. "The captain's not here. I am next in command. Tell me!"

Noah rubbed his face, as if to clear his head, and began, "The boys and girl believe a ship has been following us all the way from Ireland."

"Impossible!" Scab roared. "Your childish eyes have deceived you. All sloops resemble one another from a distance. Furthermore, I highly doubt that any collection of timber could keep pace with the *Scurvy Mistress*. What shade are her sails?"

"White," Fish answered. "Crisp and new."

"The sloop we spied off Ireland had sails that were gray as storm clouds and as weathered as old Foot's wrinkled hands."

No, he was wrong. Daniel had called out that they were white. Anyone on deck at the time could've seen them clearly.

Scab took a long drink, then tossed his mug toward the door of the Salty Scabbard, nearly hitting Foot, who was stumbling out. "I'll bet a share she's not the same, but I'll investigate."

As Scab staggered away, Noah shrugged and sauntered into the Salty Scabbard. The first mate's reaction hardly doused Fish's suspicions. In fact, it had the opposite effect. He not only believed that the sloop had followed them; he now believed that Scab was somehow involved. But it was Nora who actually proved that something was amiss, whispering, "We didn't say she was a sloop."

THE MYSTERY SHIP ANCHORED in the harbor, and that evening, Fish decided to swim over for a closer inspection. Cobb, Melinda, and Moravius were nowhere to be found, and although his friends protested, warning that he shouldn't go alone, Fish knew this was the only way to spy on that ship. Rowing the launch would be too noisy, and none of the others could swim.

His plan to approach unnoticed almost fell apart the moment he lowered himself into the water. The slightest movement of his hands or feet stirred up clouds of glowing green dots in the dark water. He'd never seen anything like it.

"Don't worry," Daniel whispered from above. "They are harmless little bugs."

Bugs? The fact that he was swimming in a sea of luminescent bugs, regardless of how beautifully they glowed, was so repulsive that he nearly climbed straight back up onto the deck. Then the sight of two figures moving in the windows of the mystery sloop's cabin renewed his resolve. Forget the bugs, Fish told himself. He had to find out more about that ship.

His hands and feet created brief, bright smears of light as he swam, but whoever was on that ship remained inside.

Not a soul was outside to spot him. Fish climbed up the anchor cable with ease—a few weeks ago it would have been a struggle, but he was much stronger now—and crept back toward the quarterdeck. The cabin door was only half open. He could barely see inside. He listened, but the wind muffled the voices.

The only words he did hear: "Cobb should burn!"

The voice he couldn't place, but that was irrelevant.

Now he knew for certain this was an enemy ship.

He had to warn the captain.

The wind rose, blowing open the door. A distinctive smell wafted toward him.

A singular mix of rotting onions and unwashed feet—Scab.

Someone stepped into the open doorway. The man was as wide and thick as Moravius, but not nearly as tall, and a single thick chain with an enormous key hung from his neck. Behind the pirate, Fish spotted two men he did not recognize and, with their backs to him, what looked like an old woman and an uncommonly small man. The door closed. His breath caught in his chest; his heart nearly stopped beating. Then Fish left as quietly as he had come.

Back on deck, he told his friends what he'd seen, heard—and smelled.

"How did they track us here?" Nate wondered.

"They could've guessed," Daniel suggested. "Risden's Isle is pretty popular."

"We have to tell Cobb," Nora said.

"What?" Nate asked. "That Fish smelled Scab on another sloop?"

Daniel noticed a launch leaving the sloop. They waited until it reached the dock, and then the four of them followed in their own ship's launch. When they reached the dock, Daniel placed his hands on one of the weathered wood planks, as if he were ready to disembark. Then he stopped himself. He pulled his hands back and exhaled.

"Come with us!" Fish urged.

"Not tonight," Daniel said. He patted the broadsides in his pocket. "But I have some reading to do. I'll see if there's anything in my papers about that pirate you described, Fish."

As Daniel rowed back to the boat, Fish, Nora, and Nate hurried to the square, where they saw one of the Tea Leaves wobbling toward them like a child learning to walk. "Ah, the blade, the future captain, and the little Irishman!"

Nate took him by the shoulders and tried to avoid the man's rum-poisoned breath. "Have you seen Cobb?"

"A moment ago, yes. Or was it last week? Ah, I forget."

Promptly, the pirate collapsed to the ground, curled his knees up to his chest, and began to snore. Fish peered through the wide-open window of the Rusty Anchor, behind the fallen Tea Leaf, and saw the huge pirate from the mystery sloop. He hoped Daniel would discover some details about the rogue.

Eventually, they found Cobb in the Salty Scabbard. Mugs flew over their heads as they entered. Beer splashed on Fish's neck. Puddles of spilled drink lay everywhere, yet Fish stomped through them unbothered. His feet had already survived much worse on board the *Scurvy Mistress*. The captain, Melinda, and Moravius were sitting at a corner table with a small, thin man with dark brown skin, round spectacles, and long fingers that tapped incessantly on the table. He wore a radiant blue tricorne hat and a fine shirt. Fish asked his friends if they knew the pirate; neither recognized him.

"The future of piracy!" Cobb proclaimed, welcoming them. He was unusually joyful and lively. "All but one of you, anyway. Where's Daniel? Refused to disembark again, eh?" He reached across the table and tapped the top of the pirate's hand. "A fascinating boy, Jameson, immensely curious, with a mind like a sponge!"

"Captain," Fish said, "we have some—"

"Manners, boy! I mean to introduce you to Captain Jameson Risden, the proprietor of this pirate utopia, a noted treasure hunter, and our . . . how do I introduce you? Would I call you a friendly rival?"

"The very best of friendly rivals!" Risden replied. "Unless we're searching for the same treasure. You're not still looking for the chain, are you?"

"And you're not scouring the seas for those emerald eyes?"

Nora glanced at Nate, then Fish. There was something about emerald eyes on Daniel's list of treasures.

"No," Risden said with a sly smile. "Of course not."

"Friendly rivals," Melinda repeated.

The pirate raised his glass. "Precisely."

"This man here is the second-best treasure hunter in all the world."

"Second best?" Risden replied.

Melinda introduced the kids quickly, and the pirates at the table bantered back and forth as Moravius listened, smiling. Fish couldn't just stand there as the storm clouds of mutiny gathered all around them, regardless of what good manners required. He appealed wordlessly to Moravius, but the giant's eyes were steeped in grog. A subtle nudge from Nora alerted Melinda to the importance of their interruption. Finally, she recognized that the kids hadn't come over for casual banter. Cobb jumped slightly—she must have kicked him under the table.

"Excuse me," Cobb said, interrupting his friend. "What is it, my friends?"

Fish started to speak, then stopped. Could this other treasure hunter be trusted? Cobb saw his concern, slipped away from the table, and pulled Fish aside, the mirth fading from his face as he asked for details.

"A new sloop sailed in today. I believe it's the one that approached as we were raiding the *Mary*. So I snuck aboard—"

"You snuck aboard? Good man!"

"Yes, and I heard a few people inside threatening to kill you."

"Our men?"

"I'm fairly sure Scab was there—"

Cobb stopped him. "You are fairly sure?"

"Well, I . . ." He knew it would sound odd, but he had to be honest. "I smelled him."

"You smelled him?"

"I know it sounds crazy, but Scab has a very distinctive odor, like old, rotten onions and—"

"Feet?"

"Yes!"

"I've noticed that myself, though I was never quite able to place the onion. But I must tell you, Fish, I need more than smells."

Fish lowered his voice. "Lady Swift and her son were with them, too."

Instantly, Cobb tensed. He glanced at Melinda, then Moravius. "Our revelries are over," he announced. "We leave tomorrow."

In the booth, Captain Risden tipped his hat to Fish, Nora, and Nate. "Perhaps our paths will cross again one day. In the meanwhile, good luck, happy hunting, and fair winds to you all."

19

The Spirit of the *Mistress*

The next morning, Cobb called the crew together on the beach. He stood in front of Moravius, who was holding the ship's flag high in the air, fastened to a cutlass, and waited until all were accounted for. Then he announced they'd be leaving by noon.

"Where to next, Captain?" Noah asked.

Jumping Jack pressed: "Will it be a raid?"

"A quest?" asked one of the Ancient Eight.

"Are you certain we can't stay?" shouted Sammy the Stomach, prompting laughter from the men.

Cobb looked directly at Fish. "We have discovered the location of a certain treasure of great value. As some of you have surmised, we seek the Chain of Chuacar. We have deduced its precise latitude and longitude, and when we arrive at our destination, we will find one of the greatest treasures ever known."

"What if it's not there?" Foot asked.

Fish thought that sort of question would've come from Scab, Jumping Jack, or Thimble. But the three of them were oddly silent.

"A perfectly reasonable query. That is one of the risks of such a quest. Our journey may prove fruitless. This is why I tell you now. I know of at least two ships anchored in the harbor that are in need of crew. I hope you will remain with us, but if you wish to leave and join another ship, that choice is yours."

Multiple men immediately and angrily announced their resignations.

Scab, Jumping Jack, and Thimble were not among these defectors. Scab acted like the dutiful mate, bound to his captain's wishes. But his performance—for Fish thought it had to be a performance—was entirely unbelievable.

The captain pointed to the hourglass on the ship's flag. "For those of you who have chosen to remain, I assure you that I understand we all must make the most of the time we are given. This is the spirit of the *Scurvy Mistress*, and I will not violate that spirit. We will commit one month to this search, then turn our minds and our swords to other endeavors should it fail. I say this now to be fair and honest, but I believe that in a short while, we will, each of us, be sleeping on pillows of gold."

Cheers resounded on the beach. At the mention of pillows of gold, which didn't actually sound very comfortable to Fish, one of the defectors turned around and rejoined the crew. For the next few hours, the pirates busied themselves purchasing knives, boots, belts, cutlasses and swords, pistols and muskets. Fish witnessed Noah haggling over the price of a fiddle and watched Sammy and the Ravenous Rovers haul off several gargantuan wheels of hard yellow cheese, cursing and complaining that the store had sold out of salami. Fish insisted on fulfilling his friend's list—a job that Melinda had always volunteered to take on herself—and Daniel had given him the necessary coins. Daniel had written out a selection of items, including a new pair of boots, a knife, and "any books, broadsides, or printed pamphlets of or relating to piracy, navigation, or the procurement of treasure." Fish went through the list item by item until he came to the last one: "New shirt for shoeless pirate."

Apparently his three friends had all chipped in, and Fish couldn't refuse the gift of a shirt that fit and wasn't ragged and worn thin. He was searching through the clothing section of Dolphin Dry Goods when he found Thimble inspecting an enormous pile of multicolored fabrics, tucking a trunk's worth under his arm. Fish successfully avoided the rogue, picked out an almost perfectly sized shirt—with a bit of room to grow into—tossed his old one aside, and paid the bill. Afterward, he rowed back to the ship with three of the Ravenous Rovers, who were so distraught to leave such fine eateries behind that they actually cried.

THE *SCURVY MISTRESS* SAILED north for several days. Nate explained that longitude was difficult to determine, so in order to sail to a particular address, they had to place themselves along the right line of latitude first, then sail east or west along that line until crossing the intended line of longitude. From Risden's Isle, this meant sailing north, then turning west for several more days before they found their destination.

The crew was nervous with anticipation. The four friends kept busy by sharing theories about the chain and imagining what they'd do with their share. They continued their research, too. Daniel had discovered a description of a pirate that matched the man they'd seen in the Rusty Anchor. His name was Gustavo de Borges, and the three most powerful nations in the world wanted him arrested on charges of piracy and theft. He was described as a tall, powerful rogue with the light, nimble feet of a dancer. According to one broadside, he was so skilled at creeping up on his victims that he'd managed to steal the queen of Spain's favorite necklace from her bedside table.

Soon a small island appeared in the morning fog. Thick trees grew to the edge of the narrow sand beach, and there were no indications that the island was inhabited, not even by a goat. Daniel said it looked like it had been lopped off the top of a mountain and dropped into the sea, while Nate thought it was really just an oversize hill. Noah, overhearing their conversation, declared it a mountill.

They approached the island's east side and circled once while Melinda sat on the quarterdeck, busily sketching a map. Fish was eager to see her rendition, but from what he could guess, the island was roughly triangular in shape, with its northernmost point turning slightly to the east. He wanted to stand with the captain and Melinda as they formulated plans, but the hierarchy of the ship needed to be respected. He was still a mere scrub, a minor deckhand, the lowest of the low. Only senior pirates were allowed on the quarterdeck at such times.

The *Mistress* anchored off the southern shore—the base of the triangle—as the sun faded over the blue-green sea. That night Fish hardly slept. All through the evening he could hear Foot grunting, Noah singing quietly to himself, Jack doing his exercises, and plenty of the others moaning and grumbling.

At dawn, a massive boot nudged him in the ribs. He tensed, thinking that Scab was provoking another fight. But it was Moravius, and he followed the giant up onto the deck and into the cabin, where Cobb, Melinda, and Daniel sat at the table. "I found the answer!" Daniel boasted.

"The answer to what?"

The captain pointed to the dozen golden coins. They were spread out, aligned in a row, with the queen's profile facing down. "These weren't decoys after all," he explained.

Daniel pointed to the letters on the coins—the ones they'd noted that night in the cabin, when Fish had first tried to help. "All along we've been assuming the message would be in English, but I've heard a dozen tongues in my time on ships! Especially Spanish, Portuguese, and—"

"French!" Cobb added.

"Walter! Let Daniel explain, please."

Daniel patted one of his note-stuffed pockets. "I was reading about a notorious French rogue when I realized these letters were not meant to form an English word at all. See this one?" he said, picking up a coin with the letters E and N. "I'd been thinking of them as two separate letters, E and N, but they're a single French word."

"A French word?"

"Look at the coins," Daniel said, pointing to the first, then pronouncing the letters on each coin in the row. "R-E-G-A-R-D-E-Z-EN-B-A-S."

This meant nothing to Fish.

"*Regardez en bas!*" Moravius exclaimed.

Fish stared at Daniel, but his friend didn't react.

Then Daniel looked at Moravius and back to Fish. "Oh, right. Now I know he speaks, too. You should've told me! But it's just the five of us, right?"

"Correct," Cobb replied. "And the two of you are the only ones who speak passable French. Translate, please."

"'Look down!'" the giant said.

"Right," Daniel added, "it means 'look down.' The

first set of coins told us how to find the island, but these tell us where on the island to look. This means the chain is buried underground!"

"Perhaps in a natural cave," Cobb added.

Fish couldn't contain his excitement—or wait to tell their friends.

Outside, the sky was turning pink. He raced to wake Nate and Nora as Moravius crowed like the world's largest, strangest rooster. The men began wandering up, eager to begin, and Cobb ordered them to make for shore in the small rowboat, six at a time. No one even bothered with breakfast.

Melinda, Moravius, and Cobb boarded the second boat, and Fish jumped in for the last trip with Nora and Nate. A few members of the crew remained on the *Scurvy Mistress*, including Sammy, Bat, Owl, Thimble, and Daniel, who wished his friends luck. Not even the lure of the legendary golden treasure could coax Daniel off the ship. Thimble's choice to remain was odd, though. Fish thought for certain he would've stayed with Scab.

Before he left, Fish pulled Daniel aside to warn him. But his friend was already suspicious. "I know," Daniel insisted. "I'll watch him."

On the beach, the crew quickly set up a small camp, gathering wood and stones for a bonfire—in case the pirates camped that night—along with water from a nearby stream. Cobb divided the crew of twenty-four into groups of four or five. He showed them Melinda's rough map and sectioned off the island, assigning each group a different area to scour. Unfortunately, Fish, Nora, and Nate were stuck with Scab and Jumping Jack.

Fish mumbled a complaint to his friends, wondering why Cobb had done that to them.

In reply, Nora whispered, "I don't think it's an accident. The captain probably wants us to watch him."

Their group had been given an area to the north, but Scab demanded a switch. "We'll take the southwest corner," he declared.

The captain eyed his first mate blankly, then agreed to the change.

"Why is this search necessary?" Noah asked. "Do you not have some idea of its location?"

"We know it is here," Cobb answered. He opened his arms wide. "As you see, this is not an outlandishly large island, but we are in search of a chain large enough to wrap around the whole of a great city."

Noah removed one of the nails from behind his ear and jabbed it in the air. "Big treasure, small island."

"Precisely. We have reason to believe it is buried underground, in a natural cave. You will be searching for the entrance."

"And if we find it?" Nate asked. "What then?"

"Fire two shots. The rest of us will follow the sound and converge there."

The crew broke off into their groups. Some proceeded down the beach in either direction; others marched forward into the island's thick brush, hacking at the leaves and bushes with their cutlasses. Fish, Nate, and Nora trailed behind Scab and Jumping Jack, who had donned a hat to keep the sun off his head. When they neared the southwestern point, the first mate stopped. "This is a man's work. We don't know what lies in that brush. You children wait here."

Nate protested. "But—"

"That's an order!" Scab barked back.

The two rogues disappeared into the trees. Nate bristled, angry at being referred to as a child. He picked up a stone and threw it at a half-submerged boulder. "This is miserable. At least in a raid I get to do something. I don't have to sit around on a beach."

"We should follow them," Nora suggested. "I still think Cobb paired us with them for a reason."

Fish agreed, and Nate led the way through the thick, overgrown brush. Flies swarmed around the young pirates' heads. Fish wiped them off his lips with the backs of his hands and swatted constantly at his neck and ears. The friends pushed on toward the western shore. Soon they crossed the southwestern point and were once again close to the water. They heard voices ahead through the brush, and all three of them dropped down. While Nate and Nora stayed back, Fish crawled ahead. Carefully, he pushed aside the branches of a dense green bush so he could see clear through to the beach. Then he swung around and silently warned his friends to move no closer.

The mystery sloop from Risden's Isle was anchored offshore. A rowboat rocked at anchor in the shore's small waves, and a rough, disheveled bunch stood talking at the water's edge: Scab, Jumping Jack, and three other pirates he didn't recognize. The strangers were predictably ragged. Each one looked like he styled his hair with the slime off a slug's back. There were two other figures among them as well. One was an unusually small man, and the other, a woman, was dressed for afternoon tea, not a treasure hunt on a remote island.

Reginald and Lady Swift had arrived.

"How did they find us?" Nate whispered.

"Scab must have told them that night on Risden's Isle," Nora guessed.

Still quiet, Nate noted, "Then Scab would've had to know the exact latitude and longitude."

Was that even possible? Before they left the island, only Fish, Moravius, Melinda, and the captain had known. Cobb would never have told Scab. So how would he . . .

Suddenly, Fish remembered that night in the cabin.

That noise outside. Had Scab been listening to everything?

Had he heard them deduce the treasure's location?

A bird flew up out of the brush, startling Fish.

He breathed. He had to keep calm. And quiet.

He listened, trying to discern what Lady Swift was saying, when another noise distracted him. Annoyed, Fish expected to see a second bird fluttering toward the sky, but his gaze fell instead on a large pair of black leather boots caked with mud and sand. He looked up. The legendary thief Gustavo de Borges stood over them, aiming one pistol at Fish and swinging the other between Nora and Nate. "Looking for something, rats?"

20

The Sight of Blood

Gustavo laughed as his mates tied Fish, Nora, and Nate to separate trees.

Scab glowered and gloated.

"Cobb will save us," Nate protested.

"That overeducated dream chaser will do no such thing!" Scab replied. "You are in the grip of Tenneford the Terrible!"

Fish hadn't heard that name before. "Who is Tenneford the Terrible?"

"I am!" Scab snapped.

"But your name is Scab."

"Not anymore. I have not had a scab in years, so that nickname is completely unjustified. I am now to be known as Tenneford the Terrible, and from this day forth I shall haunt the seven seas."

"Terribly," Nora added.

Taunting the pirate didn't strike Fish as a very good idea, but he couldn't help smiling, and he thought he heard Lady Swift chuckle.

"Not terribly," Scab clarified. "In a terrifying fashion."

This time Fish couldn't help laughing.

Scab stomped over and grabbed him by the collar. "You dare mock me?"

"We are laughing at your name, Tenneford," Nora explained. "For a pirate, it is terrible."

"My mother gave me that name!"

One of the strangers mumbled, "I told you Terrifying Ten was better. People would think you weren't merely one man, but ten!"

"Or Tenney the Terror, maybe?" Gustavo offered.

"Captain Terror!" suggested Jumping Jack.

"Yes," Gustavo agreed, "the simplest ones are often the most fearsome."

"Enough with the names!" said Lady Swift. "And enough with these three pests. I did not sail across an ocean to deal with children. I am here—"

"We, Mother," Reginald Swift interrupted.

Lady Swift rejected her son's protest. "I repeat, I am here for business, not to theorize about names or argue with junior rovers. Scab or Tenneford or whatever you choose to call yourself, hurry along so that I may procure my treasure and you your ship."

"What does she mean, 'your ship'?" Nora asked. She

nodded out to sea. "Whose ship is that? And how did you find us?"

Scab laughed. "Thimble overheard your so-called captain revealing the ship's destination back in Ireland. He dropped a note in a bottle for our friends here to retrieve, and they followed us to Risden's Isle. As for this particular destination, I overheard your talk of longitude and latitude in the cabin with Cobb and Melinda that night. Couldn't quite place the voice of the other pirate, but it's no matter. I got what I needed."

The other pirate? After a moment, Fish realized he was talking about Moravius—Scab hadn't realized the giant could secretly speak. Now he glanced back and forth between the first mate and the treasure hunter. "You've been working with her this whole time?"

"It's a unique opportunity," Scab replied.

"As for the *Mildred*," Lady Swift replied, "she is mine."

"Who names a ship *Mildred*?" Nate wondered.

"That's my mother's name!" Reginald declared.

"Enough," Scab growled. He lifted his pistol to Nora's face. "This forehead of yours, so smooth and tall, offers a delightful target."

"No!" Nate shouted.

"Wait!" Fish added. "If you fire, Cobb and the others will come running."

Grunting, Scab lowered his weapon. "The minnow is right. We cannot sacrifice our plan for this."

"Then dispose of them quietly," Lady Swift suggested. "But please wait until your men have rowed us a good way out to the *Mildred*. My delicate son abhors the sight of blood."

"Mother! I see no reason for you to announce that fact! If I'm to assume control of our operation eventually, you must allow me to deal with men of this sort without—"

"Enough!" his mother shouted. "We have treasure to find, and you want to talk of the future? If anything, your performance on this disastrous journey has convinced me that I never should have considered you a worthy heir."

Her son's face, a picture of frustration the moment before, now turned a ghastly white. "But you promised . . ."

"Promises! The only fools who keep promises are those who lack the strength to break them. Cease speaking unless you are spoken to. Otherwise, I'll have one of our hired rascals here wrap one of his filthy bandannas across your all-too-active mouth."

Broken and embarrassed, Reginald Swift did as he was told.

Fish thought he looked like he was one insult away from sobbing.

"Now, Tenneford, hurry back to Cobb's camp as we planned," Lady Swift continued. "Gustavo, I'll send the launch back to retrieve you."

"And you'll wait for my signal?" Scab added.

Lady Swift nodded. One of the other pirates, a round, redheaded man who wore dozens of necklaces, turned back to Scab and raised his cutlass. "Do you mind if I ask again . . . what is the signal?"

"Are you serious?" Lady Swift replied. "Why am I surrounded by simpletons?"

"Three pistol shots," Scab replied impatiently. "Cobb has asked for two shots from his hapless scouts. Our signal is three."

"Right," Gustavo answered. He turned to his mates. "And then we sail the *Mildred* around the coast and take the *Scurvy Mistress* while her crew is on shore."

"Thimble will dispose of the few men on board," Scab added, "so you won't have any trouble."

That explained why Thimble had remained on the *Mistress*. Scab wasn't interested in the chain. He wanted the ship. And that meant Daniel was in danger. Owl, Bat, and Sammy the Stomach were on board, too. Fish had never said more than a few words to Bat or Owl. And Sammy's only loyalty lay with his vittles. Would they help Daniel? Or side with Thimble? He tried wresting his hands free, but the bindings were too tight.

As Scab and Jumping Jack started off, Lady Swift approached Fish. "You're the messenger boy, the one who was supposed to deliver my coins."

"I am," Fish said.

"The sea has aged you. You look different now." She

touched his cheek with the back of her cold, wrinkled hand, then walked down to the waiting launch. Over her shoulder she called out to Gustavo, "Save the shoeless one for last. Rid us of the others . . . and then dispense with him slowly."

21

The Slippery Noodle

Fish struggled against the ropes. His skin burned as he tried to free his hands. Gustavo stepped toward him. The man was as thick as Moravius. The heavy chain around his neck looked strong enough to drag a boat out of the water. How the man had snuck up on them Fish could not comprehend. Fish should have at least been able to smell him. Though his breath stank more of garlic than onions and rotting feet, it nearly matched Scab's in potency.

Gustavo removed a knife and licked the partially rusted blade. His tongue was vile, reptilian. "You know what I like most about being a pirate?" he said.

"The riches?" the redheaded mate asked.

"The robbery?" the other suggested.

"Or that delightfully fresh smell of the open ocean air when—"

"Quiet!" Gustavo yelled. "Murder! The answer was murder."

"You are no pirate!" Nate yelled. "You are a coward. A real raider would allow us to fight!"

Gustavo's jaw tightened; Fish could nearly hear his teeth cracking under the strain. Then he breathed in deeply through his nose, loosening a clump of something viscous, and spat a mass of green-and-yellow gloop onto the center of Nate's forehead. He did the same to Nora, who sneered back at him without even flinching, then moved to Fish. He summoned his final phlegmatic shot from his chest, coughing it up into his mouth prior to unloading. The force of it was incredible. The glob landed in the center of Fish's forehead and stuck there momentarily before sliding gradually down toward the bridge of his nose. He wondered if it would leave a dent. If only he could free his hands! Even just one, to wipe that lung-borne slop from his face.

"Don't bother," Gustavo said, watching Fish wriggle. "You've been bound by a knot that only a few people in the world can untie."

A flash of hope sparked within him. A knot few people in the world could untie? With the fingers of his right hand, he traced the two ends of the rope, felt how they looped in, out, in again, and over. He tried to conjure a picture of the knot in his mind. It felt familiar—Gustavo had used the Slippery Noodle! On the boat, with Knot's help, Fish had tied and untied this legendary tangle dozens of times.

Gustavo spotted the gleam of one of Nora's hidden blades, a small but sharp tool tucked into the cloth she'd tied around her head. He pocketed his rusty weapon, then removed Nora's and held it up to the sun, inspecting the edge. "Ah, sharpened to perfection," he said.

Fish quickened his finger work.

The knot was loosening, but only slightly.

He needed more time.

Fish noticed the redheaded rogue caress one of his necklaces, then another, and another, closing his eyes as he did so. The pirate rubbed them as if they were prayer beads.

Gustavo pointed the blade from Nora to Nate. "Who would like to bleed first?" he asked.

"Let the other two go," Nate offered. "Those two are harmless."

"I am not!" Nora protested.

The redheaded pirate rubbed a small green figure hanging from one of his necklaces. Fish stopped working the knot and studied the pirate's jewelry. Those were not prayer beads. They were good luck charms! Charms were common enough, but most pirates wore only one or two and kept them hidden. The sheer number of this man's charms suggested he not only believed in fortune. He was obsessed.

Gustavo moved the blade toward Nate's neck.

Fish's friend was breathing heavily. His face had lost its color.

Nora was shouting for Gustavo to stop.

As his fingers worked carefully, Fish took a breath. This might be his last chance. "It's unlucky, you know."

Gustavo stopped. He pulled the knife away from Nate's skin.

"Unlucky?" the redheaded pirate asked. "What's unlucky?"

Fish tried to sound authoritative. "Everyone knows that ending the life of someone under the age of fifteen is bad luck," he answered.

The redheaded pirate placed his hand on Gustavo's wrist. "Everyone knows this?"

Breathless, Nora jumped in. "Our friend Daniel has a broadside on the subject back on the *Mistress*."

There was still a slight tremor in Nate's voice as he added, "It's true."

"If everyone knows, then why have I never heard word of it before?" Gustavo asked.

"It is . . . an Italian rule," Nora answered.

The redheaded pirate clutched his beads. He turned to Gustavo. "I don't like this . . ."

"Our orders were clear," Gustavo noted.

"She's our client, not our captain," the redheaded rogue replied.

"No intelligent scalawag would do that to an underage pirate," Nate noted.

"Otherwise, you will all be cursed with ill fortune for the rest of your lives," Nora added.

"The rest of our lives?" the redheaded pirate whispered.

"Or longer," Fish said.

"Longer?" Now his voice was so faint they could barely hear him.

"Longer," Nora repeated.

"It's not something a smart pirate does," Nate said, the fear in his voice finally fading.

Gustavo breathed in through his yellow-brown teeth. "Or I could just get it over with and see what happens . . ."

"You'd be better off leaving us here," Fish said.

"Or freeing us first and then abandoning us," Nate suggested. "That would probably bring you good luck."

"We're not fools!" Gustavo roared.

Fish glared at Nate. He had gone too far.

Gustavo began mumbling, shaking his head. The redheaded pirate was appealing to him, rubbing several of the charms around his neck.

The boat was well on its way back from dropping off the Swifts.

"So . . ." the redheaded pirate said after some thought, "if we leave you here to die, but don't kill you ourselves, is that bad luck?"

"No," Fish answered. "Not at all."

"Absolutely not," Nora added.

Exhausted by his irrational mate, the huge pirate shook his head. "Are you satisfied?" The redheaded pirate nodded. Gustavo exhaled. "That woman better pay us what we're worth. As for you three, I'd wish you fair winds, but I don't think a breeze will do you much good."

And with that, the two men turned down the beach, jumped into the just-returned boat, and began rowing out to the *Mildred*. As his friends whispered urgently about what to do next, Fish concentrated, renewing his effort. What had Knot told him? Don't force the Noodle. Pulling too hard on the wrong loop would tighten the whole. The knot had to be coaxed loose, loop by loop. The top layer had two parallel coils, which then disappeared around the bottom, moving back into the center of the knot. He spread the two parallel lines apart, inserting his index finger between them, creating just enough space to reach the intersection. Then he worked on this, reaching in deeper, feeling the whole knot loosen. One of the ends began to slip. He slid his finger through a loop and pulled it free. The first Noodle had come loose, and in a few minutes the rest followed. Fish was free. He held up his hands so his friends could see.

"How—how did you do that?" Nate stammered.

"Grab one of my blades and cut us loose!" Nora said.

He did, and soon all three of them were free, racing back through the woods. They hoped to beat Scab back to the camp, or at least arrive in time to warn the captain, but then three shots rang out through the air.

The mutiny was already underway.

22

Tenneford the Terrible

The three young pirates crawled quietly through the brush, then lay beneath a thicket of bushes at the edge of the beach. The camp was crowded; all the rest of the rogues had returned. Scab was pointing a pistol at the captain's head. Jumping Jack aimed two guns at Moravius. One of the Tea Leaves waved his cutlass near Melinda, taunting her. Scab ordered everyone but these two loyalists and their captives toward the unlit bonfire. Next to him, Fish noticed Nate growing tense, as if he was ready to charge the beach and challenge the mutineers on his own. The veins in his neck bulged. Fish placed a hand on his shoulder and whispered, "Wait . . ."

"Esteemed rogues, rascals, raiders," Scab proclaimed, "I am pleased to announce that the *Scurvy Mistress* has a new captain."

"Who?" asked Noah.

"Me, you fool!" Scab shouted. "Colleagues of mine are poised to assume control of her any moment, and from this point forward, she will sail under my command. And as captain, I am hereby declaring an end to these treasure-hunting games. The only real prize within a hundred miles is that wonderful sloop you've been wasting all these years, Cobb, and now I'm going to take her."

Cobb neglected to trace his scar; Fish guessed that, for the captain, violence now seemed like a perfectly appealing solution. His reply had the force of a cannon shot. "YOU WILL NOT STEAL MY SHIP!"

"I already have! Your days as captain are over, and the reign of Tenneford the Terrible has begun!"

Genuinely confused, Cobb asked, "Tenneford the Terrible . . . who is that?"

"I'm Tenneford the Terrible! Don't you remember, Cobb? My name is Tenneford. You're the one who started calling me Scab all those years ago. All because I had a rash that wouldn't heal. Well, I'm tired of being called Scab, Captain Corn-on-the-Cob, and I'm tired of being second-in-command to a drifting dreamer!"

The captain's face and tone turned frighteningly dark. "You . . . you . . ."

"What?" Scab said. "Say it!"

"You are a hairless boar! A leprous toe! An encrusted nostril hair, and a lice-ridden scalp!"

Scab dismissed the insults with a smile and a shrug.

"I may be all these things, but I am also the new captain of that ship," he said, pointing out to sea. "Which means that the members of your former crew have two choices. Remain here with Captain Cobb or join me and my men as we embark on a pirating adventure the likes of which the oceans have never seen. An adventure," Scab said, pausing before he added the most important point, "that will leave you wealthy beyond your wildest dreams."

Knot raised his cutlass; apparently, he had a question. Scab nodded to him.

"What about the chain?" Knot asked.

Laughing, Scab shook his head. "Don't you see? Cobb hasn't found the chain, and he isn't going to find it, either."

"But Fish and the others have yet to return. Perhaps they've discovered a clue," Knot suggested.

"All they've found is a date with the devil."

Now Cobb's voice turned quiet. "What have you done to the children?"

"I've eliminated them, and if you don't stop interrupting me, I'll do the same to you. I am trying to talk to my men. Hear these words, all of you: You will never find the chain. There is no chain. And that is why I am taking over. I have no desire to waste my best years. I want to plunder ships! We should conduct ourselves as pirates, not treasure hunters—"

Unprompted, Noah suddenly began to sing:

He's not a treasure hunter, no!
He's a pirate through and through.

The carpenter stopped as Scab pointed a pistol at his chest. The new captain stomped his foot in the sand. "You're not allowed to join us, Noah!" Scab shouted. "Your songs are tiresome! In fact, I declare that there will be no singing at all on my ship."

Several of the men booed, including Jumping Jack.

"Fine," Scab said reluctantly. "If it means so much to you, I will allow some singing. But only after sunset. And only . . . only songs about violence."

"And love?" asked Knot.

"Absolutely not!" Scab snapped.

"Maybe a few songs about rum as well?" another rogue requested.

"And meat?"

"Enough with the songs!" Scab yelled. "Now, who chooses to join me?"

Eleven men walked to his side: Knot and the three other Over and Unders; the four Tea Leaves, who openly admitted that they always sided with whoever held the most weapons; a pair of Ravenous Rovers; and one member of the Ancient Eight. Noah, Foot, and two others remained with Cobb, Melinda, and Moravius. The captain's small remaining crew cheered in his favor.

"We're with Captain Cobb!"

"Tenneford the Tiddlywinker!"

"Toadstool Tenny!"

"Tenneford the . . ."

"Yes?" Scab glowered.

The pirate who'd attempted the insult, one of the two Ancient Eight to side with Cobb, shrugged. "I don't know. I'm not very clever anymore."

In all, Scab now had a sizable crew on his side.

"And you'll leave the rest of us here to die like dogs?" Cobb asked.

"Yes," he said. "Yes, we will!"

Fish stared out at the water. The *Mildred* would arrive before too long. But for now, at least, Scab did not have control of the *Scurvy Mistress*. If Fish could get there before Scab and alert Daniel, then they might be able to save the ship. He started to back out of the brush.

"Where are you going?" Nate whispered.

"I'm going to swim out to the *Scurvy Mistress* before the *Mildred* can get there. Daniel will help—"

"Scab will get there first. You can't outrace a boat."

"So we'll stall him," Nora said.

"How?" Fish asked.

Nora winked. "Nate and I will think of something," she said. "You and Daniel save our ship."

23

Return of the Dragonslayer

Fish slipped into the sea far down the beach, out of sight. He pulled on his swimming glasses, sucked in the largest breath of his life, and plunged forward. Before long, his chest ached. When the time came to breathe, he rose up to the surface, turned, and allowed only his mouth and nose out of the water. A few breaths later he was under again. Eventually, he surfaced at the ship's stern. The *Mildred* had not yet rounded the island's western shore. Scab and his crew hadn't left the beach yet, either. Fish briefly wondered what Nora and Nate were plotting. Then he refocused on the task at hand. Fish tied his swimming glasses to his belt, climbed up the rope ladder, and crouched on the quarterdeck.

Thimble was up near the bow, apparently watching for the *Mildred*. Given that it was daytime, Bat and Owl would be sleeping. But where was Daniel? Normally he would've been sitting watch atop the mast or working on deck.

Fearing the worst, Fish crept quietly below.

As expected, Bat and Owl were wrapped in their hammocks, but so was Sammy the Stomach. Daniel was sitting back against a cannon, deep in dreamland. He'd never seen his friend sleep during the day. He started toward Daniel, hoping to wake him.

"A sleeping draft," Thimble explained.

Evidently Fish had not been as quiet as he thought. He stopped and turned to see the raider holding up a small brown bottle.

"I added it to their breakfast," Thimble explained. "Purchased it on Risden's Isle for this very occasion. And since I'm certain Scab would like to have the pleasure of ending your life, why don't we save ourselves the trouble of a mismatched scuffle? Drink what is left in this bottle"—he drew his cutlass, stepped forward, placed the bottle on the floor, and backed up again—"and you'll enjoy a small nap while I finish my work."

Behind Thimble, Fish spied a trunk overstuffed with fine linens, silks, and spools of thread. He recognized several of the fabrics from Dolphin Dry Goods. Those materials were more precious to Thimble than gold itself. If he could just distract the pirate somehow, he could hold the collection of cloth hostage . . .

Suddenly, Daniel stood up, stiffened, and shouted, "Back, dragon!"

Cutlass drawn, eyes only half open, Daniel stumbled toward Thimble. This was no time for sleep-fighting!

More annoyed than frightened, the rogue dodged him.

Fish recognized his chance. He snatched a bottle of rum off the floor, grabbed a match near Meat Pie—the nearest cannon—and raced over to the chest. He uncorked the bottle with his teeth, as he'd seen his crewmates do, dumped the rum onto Thimble's goods, and struck the match. Now he held the flame over the precious fabrics.

The pirate was aiming a pistol at Fish.

"Lower your weapon or I will drop the match," Fish yelled.

Now Thimble pointed his weapon at Daniel. "Extinguish the match or I'll extinguish your friend."

The eyes of the dreaming dragonslayer were only half open. There was no choice but to blow out the flame. And Fish was ready to do just that when his groggy, sleep-fighting friend staggered toward him. Suddenly, Daniel knocked the lit match from his hand and pushed his friend to the floor. The two of them fell behind a barrel as Thimble began screaming. The fabrics were ablaze. The red-faced pirate dropped his pistol and dashed across the room to save his precious garments.

Fish kicked the weapon out of the way, then ran at Thimble, removed his sheathed cutlass, and flung it across the cabin. Surprised, the pirate turned and struck Fish hard across the face. The man might have been thin, but there was power in that malnourished body. The blow sent Fish spinning to the deck. His cheek burned from the backhanded slap.

Then he heard an unexpected click.

Daniel was standing beside him with Thimble's pistol cocked and aimed.

He was as clear eyed and focused as ever.

Thimble eyed the weapon with profound surprise. "But I gave you a sleeping potion—"

"I don't eat breakfast," Daniel noted. "I was acting. Bat and Owl told me about my midnight dragon battles. How'd I do?"

Thimble stared at his smoldering fabrics. "Can you at least spare my threads? Those are rare Oriental silks!"

Daniel pointed to a half-filled bucket of soapy water. "Go ahead," he said, and they watched as Thimble doused the fire. The tailor looked near to tears as he picked through the sodden remains. Then he slumped back against the wall, clutching an armful of burnt silks, and turned to Daniel. "Go ahead," he said. "Finish me off."

Daniel lowered the pistol. He picked up the brown bottle. "How about a nice drink instead?" he suggested, and placed the potion near Thimble's feet, careful not to get too close.

After a resigned shrug, Thimble indulged. A pleasure-filled glaze fell over his face as he finished the bottle in a few greedy gulps. He said something about how the taste had notes of cherries and oak. His tight, hollow cheeks relaxed. His eyes began to close, then sparked open before he finally slumped to one side and dropped to the floor.

The two boys rushed up to the deck. As quickly as possible, Fish filled Daniel in on everything that had happened. Daniel, in turn, informed him that he'd decided to lie in wait and pretend to be asleep once the others had dropped off into dreamland. He wanted to see what Thimble was plotting.

"Thank you, Daniel, I—"

"You can thank me later. We have work to do."

Up top, they saw the *Mildred*. She'd rounded the isle and was heading their way.

"She's getting closer," Fish noted.

"But we still have time," Daniel said.

Back on shore, the launch remained tied in place. None of Scab's men had left yet, and neither he nor Daniel had heard any gunfire. Whatever Nate and Nora were doing was proving effective. Now it was up to Fish and Daniel to stop that fast-approaching ship and prevent its crew from boarding. But how?

"What do we do?" Fish asked. "How do we stop them?"

"You don't stop a ship," Daniel answered. "You sink it."

24

The Stomach Fires First

The one unmistakable flaw in their plan was the fact that neither Fish nor Daniel had ever fired a cannon before. The one time they'd fired a gun since he'd been on board, Fish was up on the deck and had not seen any of the process. Then again, they had Sammy the Stomach himself. Two other Ravenous Rovers had sided with Scab, but hopefully Sammy could be convinced otherwise. The boys dashed back down below. Bat, Owl, and Thimble were all snoring soundly, and they found the notoriously voracious gunner rolling from side to side beneath his hammock.

"Sammy? Sammy?"

The Stomach didn't answer. Fish shook him and splashed water on his face, but he couldn't wake the man. Yet he might be able to wake his belly.

Confident the captain would approve, given the dire circumstances, Fish hastened up into Cobb's cabin, scoured the compartments, and discovered a few cured delicacies. There was no time to slice them neatly. He tore a few chunks off the end of a salami, hurried back down, and placed the salty, fatty meat beneath the gunner's large nostrils.

"You're going to bribe him?" Daniel asked.

"In a way," Fish said. "Sammy? I have something for you . . ."

When he smelled the salty meat, Sammy sprang to life, his body and mind suddenly restored. He gorged on the snack, then stood, wobbling. "What happened?" Sammy asked, throwing his hand out against a beam to prevent himself from falling.

"We need your help."

"More salami."

Fish broke off another piece and tossed it into the gunner's gaping mouth. Sammy chewed, swallowed, and then let out a horrendous, ship-shaking belch. The smell hit Fish's nose like a fire; the hairs on his arms tingled. Sammy the Stomach slapped himself in the face several times, then asked again what had happened. As quickly as he could, leaving out all but the most crucial details, Fish told him about Scab's plan. "We need to fire on the *Mildred* before those men board our ship," he said.

"We need to sink her," Daniel added. "Can you do that?"

Fish thought the facts would be enough, but Sammy proved him wrong.

"First tell me why I should stay with Cobb," he said.

Why? Fish hadn't thought of that. Loyalty? Trust? No—neither would be enough. Thankfully, Sammy's insatiable appetite inspired a far more convincing argument. "There will be no cook," Fish said. "Nora is staying ashore."

Sammy stared longingly at the galley. "I'm with Cobb," he decided.

"Can you sink her?" Daniel asked again.

"Of course I can sink her. My appetite and my accuracy know no equals. How far is she now?"

Fish pushed open a pair of shutters so the pirate could see the *Mildred*, mainsail full, her long bowsprit pointed toward them.

"If we were to fire all four on this side—Meat Pie, Zucchini, Sausage One, and Sausage Two—it might be possible. One perfect shot could snap the mast; the other three, placed precisely, could open a large enough hole at the waterline. She'd be severely damaged, if not doomed to the depths."

Fish put his hands on the man's shoulders. "Tell us what to do."

Sammy scrunched his bulbous nose and rubbed his cheeks with vigor. The Stomach was ready to fight. "Daniel," he began, "you head up top and watch that ship. Fish, fetch me eight cartridges from the powder room and bring them here," he said. "And when you're done—"

"Yes?"

"When you're done, Fish, pour me some ale, then slice that salami properly. Those gluttonous chunks were an insult to the craftspeople who cured these meats. Feed me, follow my instructions, and I'll do the rest."

Daniel dashed up to the deck, and Sammy was ready when Fish returned with the ammunition and ale. He started ramming the gunpowder-filled cartridges down the necks of his beloved guns. "How far is she?"

"Closing."

Angrily the Stomach shouted back, "I said how far—"

Fish couldn't really guess by looking through the port-hole. He hurried and poked his head up onto the deck. "Daniel, how far is she?"

"Two hundred yards," his friend answered.

Fish rushed back down with the answer. Sammy stuffed a shot into each of the guns, opened their shutters, then called Fish over to help him roll the cannons forward, so each nose extended out over the water.

"No waves," Sammy said. "No need to account for the roll of the ship in the swells."

The pirate used a collection of tools to adjust the aim of each gun, lifting the noses and shifting them forward or aft.

Now Daniel lowered his head down through the opening, calling out, "One hundred thirty yards!"

"Where's my ale?" Sammy snapped.

As Fish ran off for a refill, Sammy walked casually from

gun to gun, petting and whispering to them. Then, one by one, starting with Meat Pie, he lit their fuses and tossed the matches into a bucket of water. The wait felt eternal, but probably amounted to no more than ten seconds. Sammy passed the time in apparent tranquility, leaning against Ham, one of the guns on the starboard side, and gulping his drink.

"A hundred yards and closing fast!" Daniel warned.

Meat Pie erupted first. The force of the shot kicked her back toward the middle of the ship, but she stopped mid-jolt, anchored fast to the deck. Zucchini blasted seconds later, followed instantly by Sausage One and Sausage Two.

Smoke filled the deck, obscuring Fish's view of the *Mildred*. He could hardly see Sammy the Stomach, let alone their target. Fish ran up top to check the results. He and Daniel cheered and threw their fists in the air. The *Mildred* was only fifty yards away now, but she wasn't drawing any closer. Her mast was cracked near the base and folded over. Her sails were dipping into the sea. Part of the deck had caught fire, and a gaping hole had been opened in the bow. The ship was already pitching forward, swallowing water. Yet her crew was not ready to capitulate so easily. Standing at the bow of the sinking ship, Gustavo began stuffing a cartridge and shot into a small cannon. The gap wouldn't be closing, but the two ships were still dangerously close. If Gustavo had any skill, he'd be able to fire directly at the boys.

Fish didn't know whether to run, duck, dive overboard, or convince Sammy to let loose a few more shots. Before the final, crucial step, however, Gustavo started fumbling through his pockets. He yelled to his mates, each of whom did the same—the pirates couldn't find a match. A frustrated and furious Gustavo moved aside as Lady Swift, her blue dress charred at the base, her gray hair a frazzled mess, stepped in front of the pirate. She removed a match from a small pocket in her once-elegant dress. Next, she struck the match against the back of her wrinkled hand and set the fuse ablaze. Then she glared across the water at Fish.

She did not speak or shout.

But he understood the message.

This shot would be for him.

25

Dueling with a Viper

Fish and Daniel dove onto the deck. One . . . two . . . three . . .

The shot whistled over their heads, punching a hole in a barrel of wine behind them. The deep red drink gushed out, staining Fish's new shirt. He was afraid to move. What if she fired again? He waited, then crawled to the railing to see.

The *Mildred*'s bowsprit was dipping into the water, her stern pointing up at the sun. The cannon was now aimed straight into the sea.

There would be no more shots fired from that ship.

The *Scurvy Mistress* was suddenly quiet. Fish heard Sammy belch. Their ship was secure, at least, but they still had to deal with Scab and his band of rogues on the beach. Fish and Daniel hurried to the starboard railing, nearest the island. Cobb, Melinda, and Moravius now stood at the water's edge. There'd been a fight, and it appeared they'd won, except for one small detail. The launch was rowing out to the ship, and Scab sat at the bow with his back to the *Mistress*, pointing a pistol at Nora and Nate.

Daniel grabbed Fish's shoulder. "We need a new plan," Daniel announced.

A ball whipped between the boys and struck the mast—a shot from a pistol.

Fish and Daniel dropped. "Where'd that come from?" Fish asked.

"Thimble?" Daniel guessed.

No—off the larboard side Fish saw Lady Swift standing upon the sinking *Mildred* with a brace of pistols hung around her shoulders. Her gray hair was swept back, her dress half soaked as if she'd fallen in the water, and she looked angry enough to light that useless cannon with her rage alone. Her son cowered behind her. Gustavo and his mates were busily loading their valuables onto their launch, abandoning ship. Despite the madness all around her, Lady Swift kept her eyes on Fish, yelling loud enough for him to hear her clearly across the water. She tossed the pistol she'd just fired and grabbed another. "There's no sense hiding, you worthless maggot!" she screamed. "I do not lose! I do not fail! The chain will be mine!"

She fired again. Daniel urged Fish to go. "I'll guard the ship," he said. "You help Nate and Nora."

"How are you going to guard the ship?"

Daniel smirked and slapped his friend on the back. "You think you're the only one who knows how to bribe Sammy?"

The two friends wished each other luck, and Fish slipped down into the water on the starboard side of the ship, out of Lady Swift's range. The launch was approaching fast. Thankfully, Scab hadn't turned to see him, and Fish stayed low in the water as he swam ahead. Nate and Nora were doing all the work, rowing hard a few hundred strokes away, urged on by Scab.

Fish slipped on his swimming glasses and dove.

A good breeze had come up, so the surface was choppy and ragged, but down below, the water was clean and clear. He swam deep, found a rock ledge about thirty yards from the starboard side, and waited. He tried to relax, but it proved impossible. His chest was screaming for air; he must have been under for a minute by the time the launch was close enough. But he couldn't surface just yet. He waited . . . waited . . . reminding himself that his friends' lives depended on him.

Finally, the boat was overhead. Fish planted his feet on an unusually smooth and flat rock lying below the ledge, on the seafloor, and pushed off toward the surface. He yanked on one of the oars first, pulling it free, then burst out of the water, grabbing the rail of the launch and pulling down hard as he took in a huge breath of air. The boat rocked. Panicked, Scab jumped up, dropping his pistol, and Fish pulled down on the rail once more.

This time it worked: The rail dropped below the water-line. A small swell rolled in, half filling the boat. With a furious cry, Scab sprang at Fish, rocking the launch enough to dump the three of them into the water.

Scab reached for Fish's neck, clamping one hand around his throat, but Fish planted both feet on the pirate's chest and pushed off, breaking free of his grip. Now Fish was out of reach, and the rascal was too uncertain in the water to swim after him. With one hand holding the half-sunken boat, Scab pulled out his cutlass, slashed at the water, and cursed. "Minnow! Squid! I'll roast you, smoke you, boil your bones!"

On the far side of the *Scurvy Mistress*, one of the cannons fired.

Fish thought he heard a plunk and a splash. Was that a miss or a warning shot? He couldn't be sure, but Daniel had clearly put the Stomach to work.

The launch was still afloat, but only barely. The rails were above the surface, but the inside was half filled with water. Nate and Nora were floundering nearby. Fish swam over to an oar that had fallen out of the launch. "Grab on!" he called to his friends. As they each took hold of one end, he pulled the other, swimming them back to the safety of the ship while Scab held on to the side of the boat, raging and screaming.

Daniel peered over the railing and dropped a rope ladder down from the deck.

Then he was gone—back to coax Sammy into another shot, Fish guessed.

Thankfully, neither Nora nor Nate were wounded. As his friends began to climb, Fish watched Scab gripping the side of the launch to keep from drowning.

"Swim over here and fight!" Scab yelled. "Fight like a pirate, you coward!"

His shouts and curses continued, but Fish ceased listening.

Let Scab or Tenneford or whatever his name was scream what he liked.

The man was no concern of theirs any longer.

His mutiny was finished.

Nora ascended first, then Nate. Fish reached the top exhausted, ready to string up a hammock and collapse for a week.

Then the ship shook as another cannon fired.

The ball splashed down into distant water with a resounding *thunk*.

Fish and his friends rushed across the deck. Gustavo and his men weren't rowing into the fight. They were fleeing, and Fish guessed Sammy had fired that last shot to help chase them away.

Triumphant, Daniel rushed up from below. At first he was smiling, but then his eyes grew suddenly wide. "Get down!" he shouted.

Fish, Nora, and Nate dropped immediately. No shot was

fired, though. Not yet, anyway. They turned to look at what had alarmed Daniel, and a soaking wet Lady Swift stood on the deck of the *Scurvy Mistress*. She was aiming a single pistol their way, and several more were holstered in the brace across her chest. Her equally drenched son stood beside her.

She sneered at Fish. "You're not the only seafarer who knows how to swim, boy, and you and your friends won't be sneaking away this time."

Fish clenched his fists. This fight had to end. Lady Swift had said that she would not fail, but neither would he. Somehow, he'd stop this treasure hunter.

He motioned to Reginald. "What about your son? I thought you shielded him from bloodshed," Fish said.

Reginald Swift winced. "I don't need your protection! I can easily cover my own eyes. And if, by this comment, you mean to imply that my aversion to the sight of blood renders me unfit for—"

"Quiet, Reginald!" Lady Swift said out of the corner of her mouth. "A good treasure hunter must do what her predicament demands. And in this case, I must eliminate you three as quickly as possible, without concern for my diminutive son's gentle nature."

"You won't be able to find the treasure without us," Daniel added.

That wasn't exactly true, but Daniel's strategy was sharp. She wanted the treasure above all else. "Daniel's right," Fish added. "We know where to find the chain."

"I don't believe them, Mother!"

"Neither do I, Reginald."

Fish turned toward the island and pointed toward the highest point.

"There's a cave," Nate said, jumping in. "We didn't tell the others . . ."

"Because we wanted to find it first," Daniel added.

"But if you let us show you the way," Fish continued, focusing on the hillside, "we could find it together."

The treasure hunter could not resist following the direction of his gaze, and this brief shift in focus was all Nora needed.

A small, gleaming knife spun past Fish in a blur.

The point of the blade pierced the sleeve of Lady Swift's right arm and pinned the fabric to the mast behind her, causing her to drop the pistol. The treasure hunter was so stunned she didn't even think there might be a second knife—and this one trapped her left sleeve to the mast before she could reach over to free her right arm.

"Don't move," Nora warned her, wielding a third knife, "or the next throw won't merely damage your dress."

A furious Lady Swift swung her red-eyed gaze toward them. Fish shrugged his shoulders innocently as Nora stepped forward, expertly tossing another of her hidden weapons into the air and catching it cleanly.

"Listen to her, Mother!" Reginald called out.

"Quiet, boy!" she snarled.

"Your son does offer good advice," Nora said. Briefly she pointed a blade at Reginald. He held up both hands and shuffled back. "Nate, would you mind tying this viper to the mast the way she had us lashed to those trees?"

"I'd be delighted," Nate answered.

Grinning, the young pirate stepped toward her. Lady Swift kicked Nate cleanly in the chest with her heel, then twisted her shoulders, trying to yank her right arm free.

The pistol! Fish lunged at the weapon, then hurled it over the railing into the sea.

Nate stumbled back, gasping.

Fish glanced over at Reginald—he'd backed away even farther.

Finally, Lady Swift pulled one arm free, then the other. "That's the sternum," she explained, pointing one of her wrinkled fingers at Nate. "He'll find his breath in a moment." She eyed Nora, who wielded another blade, ready to throw. Lady Swift held up her hands, palms out. "Put down your weapon, dear, and I promise to leave peacefully. These shipboard scrums are below me."

Daniel eyed Reginald. "What about you?"

"Him?" Lady Swift replied. "He will do as I say. He's like his father. Willing to share in the spoils, but useless in the quest for them!"

Now Reginald straightened. "That's enough!" her son yelled back. "It was not my fault the coins were stolen! And it is not my fault these kids outsmarted you! I am tired of your constant criticism!"

"Criticism sharpens a dull blade, Reginald."

"I'm not a dull blade!"

"No, you're a delicate and diminutive flower, and as for these urchins outsmarting me," she said, "I hardly think that is true. Yes, I am conceding the fight today. Here, on this ship. But victory? The chain? Both will soon be mine. If you do know where to find the chain," she said, turning to Fish, "then I'd encourage you to do so quickly, gather as many pieces as you can, and then flee for your miserable lives. More of my allies will be arriving soon," she added, "and these friends do not cower in the light of cannon fire."

More friends? He guessed she was lying, but Fish would have to warn Cobb.

As Nate rose to his feet, Nora grabbed his hands, gazed into his glassy eyes, and embraced him. Nate wrapped his arms around her, too.

"I—" Nate started.

Nora shyly pulled away. "Me, too—"

"Young love, how heartwarming," Lady Swift said with a smirk. "I could say that you will enjoy decades of delightful companionship, but marriage is never delightful, and, more importantly, I believe your hours on this earth are limited."

Behind him, Fish heard the unsettling click of a pistol being readied to fire.

26

A Pistol Would Be Too Quick

Scab stomped across the deck, soaked through and angry as a taunted bull. He stuck the tip of his tongue through one of the hoops in his lip. His dark eyes and thick veins pulsed with hatred. Yet there was a kind of joyful anticipation in his face, too. The man was excited.

"H-how—" Fish stammered.

Thimble stumbled out from behind a barrel holding Nate's bow. "I fired a line to the launch, and he pulled himself in," the pirate explained. His words were slightly slurred as he turned to Daniel. "It'll take more than a few glugs of that sleeping draft to put me down for the day."

With her ally aboard, Lady Swift was revived. "Did you enjoy my little speech?" she asked Fish and his friends. "I meant every word, but it did serve its purpose." She sat atop an upright barrel, making herself comfortable, then smiled with anticipation, as if she were preparing to watch a sporting match or a stage play. "I expect I'll enjoy this thoroughly."

Scab pointed his pistol at Fish. Then he glanced at his gun and shook his head. "No, a weapon of this sort would be too quick. I prefer to see you perish gradually from a thousand small cuts." The pirate tossed his weapon to Lady Swift. "See to it that the rest of these children do not interfere. This is personal. This is between me and the minnow."

With that, Scab rushed at him.

Fish jumped out of the way, tumbled, sprang to his feet.

Scab lunged at him again, cutlass drawn. Fish grabbed his swab, held it with both hands, and blocked Scab's blows with the handle. He deflected a strike aimed at his left side, stepped back, knocked away another swinging toward his right, then ducked. The rusting blade nearly trimmed the top of his head. He actually felt the metal move through his hair.

"Know where you are!" Daniel called out to him. Then he pursed his lips as Lady Swift aimed the pistol his way.

Over his shoulder, Fish spotted the puddle of spilled red wine. He backed up, kept his eyes on Scab, and baited the rogue into charging at him. At the last instant, Fish stepped aside and swung his swab at the pirate's ankles. Scab slipped in the puddle and fell to the deck.

Daniel, Nate, and Nora cheered.

But Scab was up again quickly.

He licked the wine off the flat of his blade.

"Keep moving," Daniel reminded Fish.

"Filet that flounder!" Lady Swift yelled.

"Quiet!" Scab roared back.

The pirate moved in close—too close. Fish couldn't afford to make the same mistake as the last time, trapping himself against a barrel with nowhere to run.

If he was going to defeat Scab, he'd have to exhaust him.

He had to keep moving.

Fish sprinted up to the quarterdeck, dodging a punch to the head and several stabs from the cutlass. Frustrated, Scab threw the blade aside and leaped at him, but Fish was too fast. Daniel, Nora, and Nate each tried to help once or twice, but Fish himself called them off.

This was between him and Scab.

And he needed to win this fight his way. He ran back down to the deck, then up again, using the handle of the swab as his sword. Fish blocked, ducked, dodged, and dove out of the way as he and Scab circled the boat five, six, seven times. Scab was tiring, but he had an endless store of tricks and tactics, too. The ruthless rogue stomped on Fish's bare foot up near the bow, crushing his toes. Fish ignored the pain. He ran for the stern before Scab could take hold of him. At the top of the stairs to the quarterdeck, the pirate drove his sodden boot into Fish's chest.

His balance gone, Fish fell backward, thumped his head, and then rolled down the steps like a barrel.

Lady Swift cheered. "Hooray!"

Fish climbed up to one knee. His eyesight was blurred. Daniel and Nora rushed to him, but he called them off again.

"This is between me and the minnow!" Scab growled.

Fish watched Scab coming toward him, but the pirate was shimmering, as if he were underwater. There was a sharp pain in the back of his head and neck. Yet he'd be finished if he remained there. He had to move!

He forced himself up and sprinted to the bow.

Gradually, his vision was clearing.

Fish not-fought, dashed back to the stern, not-fought some more.

He engaged and hurried away again and again.

Scab chased him madly all the while.

A stumbling Thimble nearly got in Fish's way once, but Daniel shoved the tailor aside.

When Nora held up a blade, as if ready to throw, Lady Swift aimed the pistol her way.

Reluctantly, Nora pocketed her weapon.

Although he appreciated her efforts, Fish didn't need her help. This was his not-fight. Fish would defeat Scab his way, without a weapon, and without throwing so much as a punch of his own.

The plan was working, too. The pirate's frustration

was increasing. His breathing was labored. With every dodged blow, Scab grew angrier. His face was as red as blood.

On the quarterdeck again, Scab took up his cutlass and swung at Fish's midsection. Fish held out the swab to block it, but Scab's blade severed the handle and sliced a shallow cut across his stomach.

Again, Lady Swift cheered with delight.

Fish glanced down at the slight wound.

He'd endured worse.

Yet it was too much for Reginald. His mother hadn't been exaggerating. The tortured treasure hunter fainted, and the sound of the man collapsing to the deck briefly stalled the fight.

His mother didn't rush to his aid. She merely shook her head in disappointment.

Nora capitalized on this brief distraction, hurling another blade.

The knife struck the pistol in Lady Swift's outstretched hand.

The weapon dropped to the deck, and Nate rushed over to retrieve it. The sight of blood may have dropped Reginald, but it renewed Scab. The pirate slashed his cutlass with absolute fury. Still, he was tiring. Scab bulled after Fish, trying to land kicks to his chest, but he only struck air. Soon his thrusts started to become slower and heavier. Scab's breathing grew more and more laborious. Even his curses lost their power. "You spineless . . . sardine . . . soft-shell crab . . . slow-swimming . . . sea turtle."

Finally, Scab ceased running. He stuck the tip of his cutlass into the deck and leaned on the hilt as if it were a cane. The mutinous mate could barely stand.

"Give up, Scab," Daniel added. "The fight's over!"

Lady Swift taunted him. "Find some courage, Tenneford! You're being beaten by a child!"

"Finish him, Fish!" Nate yelled.

He knew what that normally meant for a pirate, but Fish had no intention of killing Scab. And he would not allow anyone else to, either. He'd backed up against the starboard side of the ship. The launch was within reach below; the small boat remained laden with water. An idea occurred to Fish. *Know your surroundings,* Daniel always said. If Fish could time it right, the move might work.

"You want the *Scurvy Mistress*?" he said to Scab. "You'll have to get rid of me first."

This single, simple taunt was enough. Scab summoned the last of his energy, clenched his leathery fists, and let out a guttural, animal-like roar. He reached into the folds of his shirt, removed a jagged, bloodstained knife, and charged forward. Fish waited until Scab was merely a step away. Then, just as Daniel had taught him, Fish reached out and clasped the pirate's knife hand, dropped to a crouch as he moved to the side, spun, and pulled the knife toward where his chest had been, using the rebel's momentum against him. The pirate, blade extended, was now leaning out over the railing with his knife in thin air, stunned that it hadn't found flesh. Fish moved behind him and, with all his strength, pushed Scab over the edge. The exhausted rogue landed with a splash beside the barely floating launch.

A cheer rang out. His friends were the source this time, though—not Lady Swift. Daniel joined him at the railing. Nora and Nate, too.

Meanwhile, down in the water, a stunned and exhausted Scab had managed to grab hold of the launch.

"He needs a crew," Nate said, wielding the pistol. "Lady Swift?"

The treasure hunter slid down from her seat atop the barrel, straightened her posture, and called to her son, who was now sitting upright. "Let's go, Reginald. You've had your nap." As she walked regally across the deck, her son remained in place. Lady Swift stepped up onto the railing, then stopped and smiled at Fish. "Tell your captain that he's won the day, but not the prize."

Then she plunged down into the water beside the launch.

Fish heard Nate calling to Thimble. Naturally, Scab's weaselly ally had tried to slip away. Now Daniel and Nora steered him to the railing.

"I can't swim," he announced. To Fish, he added, "You'll have me drown, then?"

"You'd let us drown," Nate noted.

Yes, but that was no reason to do the same to him. Daniel suggested they lower the rope ladder, and Thimble climbed down without complaint, clutching his remaining precious fabrics under one arm. "There was a ladder?" Lady Swift muttered.

Scab hardly registered their arrival. Only a foot or so of the small boat remained above the surface. With a little work, though, the launch would safely keep them afloat. Fish tossed down a bucket so they could bail out the water. He wanted them to drift, not drown. Against Nate's protests, Daniel sent down some fresh water and hardtack. They'd likely drift for days before finding land or another passing ship.

At the railing, Reginald Swift peered down at his mother. His face was pale.

"Reginald! Get down here now!" his mother called up.

Her son gathered his breath and straightened his back. "I intend to stay," he replied. He looked from Fish to Nora, Daniel, and Nate. "If you will allow it."

"Absolutely not!" Nate said.

"Cobb would not approve," Nora added.

"But he could be useful," Daniel noted with a shrug.

"I will do anything," Reginald pleaded. "Anything, so long as I can escape from underneath my mother's thumb. I'll swab the decks, cook . . ."

Anything? Fish wondered. There was one task he'd

gladly pass on to someone else, if he could. "Would you scrub the seats of easement?"

Without pause, Reginald Swift, who only moments before was the likely heir to an immensely profitable treasure-hunting venture, solemnly nodded his head. The most vile task on the ship was preferable to continuing as his mother's minion. "I would and I will."

Daniel extended his hand with a smile. "We'll need the captain's approval, of course, but I think we can secure that role for you."

"Welcome to the *Scurvy Mistress*," Fish added.

"But, Reginald!" Lady Swift cried up to him. "Do you intend to let me drift off into oblivion with these . . . scoundrels?"

"I worry more for the scoundrels, Mother. You'll survive. But I won't, not if I remain at your arm. Good-bye," he said. "I have excrement to clean."

Nate directed Reginald to the nearest seat, and Daniel and Fish watched Scab closely. He was not one to capitulate easily, and, given time to recover from the fall, he'd once more be ready to fight for the ship he craved. The three castaways clung to the side of the drifting launch. Thimble was reaching over the rail and slowly emptying buckets full of water out of the bottom. Meanwhile, Lady Swift watched the horizon with a crooked, almost amused smile. What was she looking for? Fish wondered. And what did she mean when she'd mentioned her friends? The treasure hunter gazed up at Fish from the water. He could read her lips easily enough as she reminded him of her message for Cobb. "The day," she said, "not the prize."

As the small boat coasted away in the current, drifting one hundred yards, then two hundred, with Thimble steadily emptying one bucket after another, Scab revived, unleashing a storm of curses the likes of which Fish had never heard. "You rotten carp! I'll drown you in Cobb's blood! I'll char you over an open fire! I'll use the shards of your broken bones to pick my teeth!"

Fish stopped listening to the failed mutineer.

The reign of Tenneford the Terrible was over.

Fish climbed up to the quarterdeck, took out a spyglass, and spotted Gustavo and his mates adrift in the current as well, their launch piled high with their remaining belongings. On the beach, the captain and the navigator were standing at the water's edge, staring out at the *Scurvy Mistress*—Cobb and Melinda were safe. Moravius loomed behind them, and their former captors were now prisoners themselves, lashed together near the unlit bonfire with two of the Ancient Eight standing guard. Or sitting, actually, Fish realized. The old pirates must have been exhausted from the fight.

He'd have to swim ashore to give Cobb the news, now that the launch was gone. First, though, he allowed himself a moment to rest. He leaned against a railing and stared out at the endless blue sea. He could still hear Scab's shouts, but the rogue's curses mingled with the sounds of the wind rushing over the deck, the tiny waves splashing up against the hull. Though it was not his place—or not yet, anyway—Fish was comfortable up there on the quarterdeck, gazing out to sea from his new home.

27

Forgotten Fish

Fish's friends rushed up to join him on the quarterdeck. Nora and Nate were eager to hear how Daniel and Fish had thwarted Thimble, and the two boys begged their friends to recount their adventure on the beach. "How did you two stall Scab?" Daniel asked.

"Wasn't I," Nate answered. "Nora proved to be the mastermind."

"What *were* you planning to do, Nate?" she asked.

"I don't know . . . fight them?"

Nora shook her head. "I assumed as much, which is why I charged out ahead of you. We weren't going to prevail in a fight. I figured the only way to slow Scab was to turn his men against him, to discourage them from leaving."

"How'd you manage that?" Daniel asked.

With a smile, Nora shrugged. "I announced that we'd found the chain."

"But why would you—" Fish started, then stopped himself. If the men believed Nora and Nate had discovered the treasure, they wouldn't have wanted Scab to sail away, even if they were on his side. They'd want the gold first. "That's brilliant!" Fish said.

"Very shrewd," Daniel added.

As a sort of thank-you for the compliment, Nora bowed. "The mind is sharper than the sword, right, Fish? Of course, Scab was suspicious," she added. "We were supposed to be dead. But the rest of the men didn't know that. They just wanted to know where to find their treasure."

"Nora told Scab and the rest that we had cut through the woods to get back here faster and stumbled upon the entrance to a cave en route," Nate recalled.

"I knew you needed time, Fish, so I described, at length—"

"At *great* length," Nate added with a laugh.

"I described at great length what we'd supposedly seen," she continued. "I invented a small tale about an underground cave, and we told them you were waiting at the entrance for us to return. The men were convinced. You could see it on their grimy faces; they looked as though they could all but touch the gold."

"Scab tried to convince them we were lying," Nate said, "but they wanted to see for themselves. If he'd tried to make those men leave, he would have had his own mutiny on his hands. To be honest, I think even Cobb himself believed Nora."

"You are quite the storyteller, Nora," Daniel noted.

"Yes, well, despite Scab's protests, the men were already starting to argue over who'd go back with us to check the cave," Nate continued, "when we heard the *Scurvy Mistress* fire. Scab knew right away that something had gone wrong."

"Scab turned to aim his pistol at Cobb—"

"And then Moravius struck!" Nate interrupted excitedly.

Nora glared at him. "I thought I was the storyteller."

"Right, my apologies. Proceed."

"Moravius picked up this fallen tree trunk as if it were as light as a swab, swung it, and felled half a dozen of those dastardly turncoats," Nora continued. "Unfortunately, Scab ducked, fired his weapon, then took the two of us hostage. The giant took a shot in the shoulder."

A bolt of concern coursed through Fish. "How badly is he wounded?"

"I'm sure he's survived much worse," Daniel replied. "That would be the third time he's been shot in the years I've been on the crew. We should check on them, though, and let them know the ship is safe. I'd row ashore myself, but . . ."

"I know," Fish replied. "No launch. I'll swim."

"While you're doing that, we'll see about cleaning up some of this mess," Daniel said, noting the condition of the deck, which was littered with overturned barrels and spilled wine.

Exhausted from the fight, Fish swam slowly, but Cobb, Melinda, and several others were waiting at the edge of the water when he approached. He hadn't even pulled off his goggles when he declared, "The *Mistress* is safe, and Scab is gone."

The pirates cheered the good news—or most of them, anyway. The mutinous allies of Scab had been bound to trees at the edge of the beach as punishment for their treachery. One of the Ancient Eight sat on a stone near Knot. Fish guessed that Cobb had ordered the added watch since tying up Knot was pointless. Melinda and Cobb immediately began peppering Fish with questions. First, though, Fish wanted to know about Moravius. The gargantuan pirate was up and moving, but doing so carefully. "How bad is the wound?" Fish asked.

"He'll be fine," Melinda replied, backing Daniel's assertion. "He's resilient."

The pirate reassured Fish himself, offering a quick and subtle wink, and Fish proceeded to summarize what had happened. The captain was disappointed to learn that Nora's story about finding the treasure was a strategically concocted fiction, but he was thrilled to hear that Fish and his friends had sent Scab, Thimble, Lady Swift, and her band of pirates drifting to the distant horizon. Once Fish had recounted the essential details, Cobb declared that they could talk more later, as a crew. First, he said, there was work to do. Guided by the incomparable boatbuilding genius of Noah, and the efforts of Cobb's remaining crew of loyalists, the stranded pirates managed to construct a rudimentary raft in record time. Fish swam one more round trip to the boat to fetch Noah's tools, then hurried back to help his friends clean. Before long, the rest of Cobb's allies were rowing out to the *Mistress* in small groups.

As they settled aboard, Cobb ordered a grand celebratory feast. Nora hurriedly prepared the meal of her young life, using the finest foods on board, including all the best provisions from the captain's newly replenished private stock, and all free hands finished cleaning the deck. Noah fashioned a long dining table made from spare planks and surrounded it with barrels to serve as seats. Before long the table was piled with charred chops, boiled ham and vegetables, hunks of cheese, potatoes, and bacon, plus pitchers overflowing with ale and fresh island spring water.

Cobb, Melinda, and Moravius clustered at one end, with Nora, Nate, Daniel, and Fish across from them. Noah took a spot in the middle, flanked by an Ancient Eight and a Ravenous Rover. Sammy the Stomach, Bat, Owl, and Foot filled out the other side. The meal was absolutely incredible—Fish ate enough for three—and it felt right and good to be enjoying it on the ship. They could have eaten onshore, but knowing that some crew members had land-sickness, Cobb insisted they all celebrate their victory together on the *Scurvy Mistress* herself.

Halfway through the meal, Noah stood up from the table, fidgeted with the pencil behind his ear, then clasped his hands behind his back, adjusted his ponytail, and sucked in his potbelly.

The captain called for silence, and the carpenter began to sing:

> *He's Fish the swimming pirate,*
> *His first mate is the sea.*
> *Ask that boy to walk the plank*
> *And he'll leap straight off with glee.*
> *Blades might clash*
> *And pistols pop,*
> *His life may be at risk,*
> *But Fish won't swing*
> *A single blade*
> *Nor even raise a fist.*

Noah paused to gather his breath.

"What about Daniel?" Nora asked.

"We couldn't have done it without Nora and Nate, either," Fish added.

After a mild belch, Sammy added, "I'd like a verse myself."

"It's my first draft!" Noah protested. "Can we get on with it, please?"

The pirate swept out his arms and began slowly, signaling everyone to join in the chorus, and they sang one more round of the newly written shanty as each pirate—save Moravius—bellowed louder than the next. When they were done, Fish wasn't sure whether he wanted them to forget the song forever or belt out the chorus just one more time. It felt strange to be hailed a hero. He didn't know how to respond to their smiles and cheers, so he busied himself with a new pile of potatoes.

"This meal is positively royal, Nora! The great kings and queens have never eaten so well. Mr. Swift!" Cobb called out. "More libations, if you please!"

As Nora smiled proudly, the diminutive man hurried over with half a dozen bottles under his arm.

"Wonderful, Mr. Swift. You are doing a very, very fine job. In fact, you may now consider yourself an official member of our esteemed if shorthanded crew."

Reginald Swift abruptly bowed, causing his large glasses to fall to the deck. He placed them back on and bowed again. "I am honored. And I thank you for the compliment, sir," he said. "I've never had anyone praise my work. I admire the way you lead your crew, Captain Cobb."

"Thank you, Mr. Swift, and you are very welcome."

"Have you had a chance to sample any of this delightful fare?" Melinda asked.

"No," he answered, turning stoic. "The seats of easement require my attention."

As the reborn Reginald Swift hurried off to his duties, Fish struggled to stifle a smile.

Next, Cobb thanked Daniel for what must have been the tenth time since he'd returned to the ship, applauding his ability to outwit the exceedingly clever Thimble. Then Fish asked Nora and Nate to tell them all, again, how they'd stalled Scab with the story about finding the cave. But Nate was quick to change the subject and highlight Fish's heroics. "When we were in that boat with Scab," he recalled, "we didn't know what was going to happen next. We figured we'd all be doomed."

Nora raised her mug of water. "Neither of us expected Fish to strike from below!"

"Nor did Tenneford the Terrible!" Melinda joked.

The group cheered again and raised their mugs, but Fish did not join them. Nora's words had brought him back down below the surface, to the moment before he swam up beneath Scab's boat. The pain in his chest returned, as if he were still holding his breath, and he recalled an observation he'd made at the time. It wasn't even a full thought, really, just something odd he'd noticed about the rock he'd pushed off to swim up toward the boat. He remembered, in that instant, being surprised that it felt so smooth and flat, almost as if it were polished.

Could that have been—

He shot to his feet, nearly upending the makeshift table. "What is it?" Cobb asked.

"The gold coins," Fish blurted, almost too excited to speak.

"What of them?" Cobb asked.

Fish turned to Daniel. "They say to look down, right?"

"*Regardez en bas*," Melinda noted.

"That's right," Daniel replied. "Why?"

"Well, they had fish on them, too. Don't you see?"

Daniel hurried to the railing. He pointed over the side of the ship, then glanced back at Fish. "Look down?"

"I don't understand," Cobb said.

Moravius lifted a hand to his forehead; his eyes widened.

Melinda glanced at Daniel, then Fish. "You don't think—"

"What if the chain is not on the island at all?" Fish asked.

"What if we're not looking *down* in the right place?" Daniel added.

Cobb pointed at the swimming glasses tied to Fish's belt. "There is only one way to find the answer."

Fish needed no further encouragement. Seconds later, he was back in the water, fixing his glasses over his eyes and preparing for a dive. He tried to guess where he'd positioned himself before so that he might locate the same ledge and the same strangely smooth and flat rock. But if his theory was correct, then what he was searching for wouldn't be all that difficult to find. He wouldn't need to be in a precise spot. Beneath the surface, he saw a long line of identically sized and shaped rocks extending far in either direction. The arrangement was unnatural. The line was interrupted only where the sunken *Mildred* had settled down to the floor. Otherwise, it wove between the beds and branches of coral as if every piece had been purposefully placed. Each of the strange rocks looked to be linked to the next.

He kicked down to the bottom, swept the sand off one of the stones. Right there, beneath him, lay an enormous block of gold. Clusters of seagrass grew on and around it, but he was sure it was gold. He tore off the greenery and saw that the gold was inlaid with blue and purple stones. He turned in one direction, then the other. This was no trick of the light. This was no illusion. Large, bejeweled blocks of gold wrapped around the whole of the island like a chain around some giant queen's neck. He had found the Chain of Chuacar.

His starved lungs were screaming for air, but he couldn't kick back to the surface. Not right away. For at least a moment more, before he swam up to tell the others, he would stay down there, at the bottom of the sea, alone with his discovery. This was where he belonged. He was no farmer. He was no messenger boy. He was a treasure hunter in a sea of gold.

28

A Very Good Problem

The four friends sat on the railing as the moon rose higher in the sky. Nearly all the other pirates were singing, drinking, and carousing around the deck. Aside from Foot, who was busily calculating the value of all the gold in the great chain, the young treasure hunters were the only clearheaded members of the crew remaining. Fish wasn't sure if their shipmates would ever tire of celebrating. Yet he wasn't about to protest. He was just as thrilled. They'd actually found the Chain of Chuacar! The muscles in his face hurt from all the smiling, and his mind was filled with wonderful waking dreams. What would his parents say when he sent home his share? What about his brothers and sisters?

Fish wasn't the only one dreaming. Nora, Daniel, and Nate had already begun talking about what they might do with their new riches. Daniel was going to purchase his parents a grand house on a hill. Inside, there'd be a library with shelves so high that he'd need a ladder to reach the top rows of books. His land-sickness? He'd find a way to overcome the stubborn ailment if it meant spending time in a library like that. Nate planned to save his share, but for what he wouldn't say, and Nora wondered if her earnings would be enough to buy a fine home in a city like London or Paris. One staffed with a butler, maybe, and someone to clean, but no chef! She planned to do the cooking herself. And in a real kitchen, no less.

When the kids finished detailing their dreams, the wind calmed, and they sat in silence, watching the water. Then Fish noticed that Daniel was watching Foot. His friend was squinting, studying the purser intensely. "What is it?" Fish asked. "Is something wrong?"

"No, not exactly," Daniel said. "But I was watching Foot tally our haul, and I was thinking . . ."

"You were thinking what?" Nora pressed.

Daniel squinted at the water. The boat had swung around at anchor with the change in the tide and current, but he was looking in the general area of the spot where Fish had found the first golden block in the chain. "You said the blocks you spotted were all identical, right, Fish?"

Fish nodded. "That's right." After his discovery, he'd come up for air, then plunged back down, swum along the bottom, and seen at least a dozen more of the blocks quite clearly. Countless others appeared to extend into the distance. "Each one was huge," he added. "On one of my dives, I planted my feet in the sand and tried to move one, but it wouldn't even budge!"

"Right," Daniel said. "That's what concerns me."

"Why would a huge block of gold upset you?" Nate replied with a laugh. "The bigger the better!"

Exactly, Fish thought. What was bothering Daniel?

Now Nora suddenly became worried. "Oh . . ."

"What is it?" Fish asked.

"Well," Daniel replied, "if the blocks were so heavy you couldn't even move one, then how are we going to get them off the seafloor?"

"Oh," Nate replied, his mirth fading.

Fish hadn't thought about that; Daniel raised a great question. Then again, they had some of the smartest, most resourceful people he'd ever met in their crew. Fish was certain either Moravius, Melinda, Cobb, Noah, or one of the others would devise a solution. He wouldn't be surprised if Daniel himself figured out what to do—he could see his friend's mind working already. The size of the blocks was an obstacle, yes. But they'd overcome much greater difficulties before. And he was sure they'd do it again. "Yes, that is a problem," Fish added, "but it's a very good problem to have."

ABOUT THE AUTHOR

GREGORY MONE IS THE author of the *New York Times* bestsellers *Bill Nye's Great Big World of Science* and the Jack and the Geniuses series (with Bill Nye), as well as the acclaimed *Atlantis* duology.

He loves the water as much as Fish, but admits he wouldn't have survived very long on a pirate ship. This story was inspired by the complex treasure hunts he used to set up for his family. He lives with his wife and three children on Martha's Vineyard.

Read on for a sneak peek at

Fish's next adventure!

The Duke's Curse

The harbor was burning. Fish thought it looked as if the sea itself had caught fire. The few remaining ships anchored in the once peaceful waters of Risden's Isle were now floating bonfires. The attack had been brutal, swift, and total. An initial, lone shot from the distance had been followed by dozens more, and Fish, Nora, Moravius, and the remains of their rapidly shrinking crew had stood frozen in the sand, watching the terrible scene.

Nora grabbed him just above the elbow. "She's not here," Nora said. "Thank the stars."

The *Scurvy Mistress* must have slipped out of the harbor before the onslaught. "Thank Daniel and Sammy," Fish replied.

"We should make our way to the other side of the island," Nora suggested.

Fish repeated the suggestion aloud for the others, and the rest of the pirates needed no further orders. Immediately they turned and started back into the woods. Yet Nora, Moravius and Fish couldn't pull themselves away.

The scattered fires, combined with the dull moonlight forcing its way through the clouds, provided enough light for them to see with some clarity. The tide had turned slack. The current had stalled, and a ship was coasting slowly through the narrow entrance to the harbor. Three masts rose from its wide decks. Thin trails of smoke rising from the sides of the ship suggested an intimidating array of cannons. The way the smoke enveloped the ship made it seem as if this boat hadn't drifted in from the open sea at all, but from some other world entirely—a world even more devastating than the burning waters around them.

The mystery ship moved in closer. The air cleared. At the bow, Fish made out two figures. The first and foremost he did not recognize. She was tall and well-dressed, with a high-collared coat, a wide sash tied around her forehead, and hair swept back over her shoulders. The way she loomed over the bow suggested she was the captain, and she brandished an enormous gleaming sword better suited for the long-gone world of armored knights. Beside this strange figure, Fish was sickened to see a small, squat man. The sight of that vile rogue made him feel like he'd been punched in the stomach.

"That's Scab," Nora said. She turned to Fish. An

unfamiliar spark flashed in her eyes. A glint of rage. "Maybe Nate was right," she snapped. "Maybe you should've—"

His friend didn't finish her thought. One of the cannons at the bow of the brigantine spewed fire, and a flaming ball spun toward them through the sky. Fish and Nora leaped in opposite directions. Moravius didn't budge. The shot soared far over their heads and landed in the abandoned town square.

Now, for the first time, Fish heard cries in the distance. Splashing, too. Never mind what Nora meant by that half-finished remark—someone was in trouble. Near a burning sloop he spotted arms flailing and splashing, and Fish was off the sand and into the water before Nora, Moravius, or anyone else could stop him. He churned through the harbor as fast as his arms and legs would allow. Small fires burned all around him. Sections of the different ships had been blown away in the attack, and many of these floating remains were alight and drifting. Slowing his pace, he raised his head higher, trying to spot the drowning victim. Finally, he spotted a single pale hand reach out of the water as if grasping for a rope. He dropped his head and sprinted again. The drowning victim would be going under soon, if they hadn't gone down already, and Fish had to save the poor soul before it was too late.

He swallowed a few deep breaths and dove. The light from the flames above shined through the otherwise dark sea. Still, he could only see a few feet in front of him. He hadn't taken the time to put on his swimming goggles but wasn't sure they'd do much good anyway. He stretched wide with each pull, hoping his hands might brush up against the sinking victim. Yet Fish felt only water. Desperate for air, he raced to the surface, sucked in several huge breaths, and dove again. This time he swam in wide circles, spiraling his way down toward the bottom. He'd spent enough time diving in these waters the last time they'd been on Risden's Isle to know he'd need to pressurize his ears once to reach the harbor's floor. Now he felt the need coming on, the dull ache building in his ears and head. He pinched his nose and blew out. The relief was immediate, and he dove deeper. His air was running short again, though, and he was nearly ready to rise for a breath when his right hand grazed what felt like skin. He turned immediately, pulled, and kicked down. Finally, he found his target. An arm first—he grabbed a thin wrist scattered with rope bracelets. The victim didn't move initially, then seemed to be jolted with the spark of life. Fish made straight for the surface, gripping with all his might as he pulled with his one free hand and kicked mightily.

Yet the person wasn't moving.

His victim pulled free of his grip, then grabbed Fish around the ankle and yanked him down. Fish tried to kick free. He used his other foot to strike down at his attacker, but it was no use. Whoever was grabbing him was small but incredibly strong. There was no chance of Fish fighting his way free of their grip. So he stopped resisting. He relaxed. He let his mystery assailant pull him deeper, and when he finally felt that grip relaxing in response, he kicked down and pulled up the knee of his opposite leg just as quickly.

His foot was free. He raced for the surface, broke through, and breathed in the smoky air.

Two swimmers emerged nearby from the water. A man and a dark-haired girl whose wrists were covered with bracelets. Fish treaded water, watching them. Neither looked close to drowning; they seemed perfectly comfortable in the water. Suddenly the man dove. Fish felt movement below him, and then a long and hairy arm wrapped over his shoulder and chest and pinned him tight. Fish gasped and tried again to wrestle himself free. Yet he couldn't escape the man's grip. The man loosened but didn't release his hold, and the girl, treading water, stared back at them. She'd pretended to drown to draw him out there. But why? She couldn't have been much older than Fish himself. Her skin was pale, her hair black and short. Turning, she waved to someone in the distance. Again he tried to escape the grip of the man holding him across the chest, but the effort was wasted. Fish was on his back as the man churned ahead through the water, pulling Fish with him, and the girl trailed close behind.

"Don't bother fighting him," she warned. "He can out grapple a shark."

The remark was meant to be a warning, Fish realized,

yet it didn't so much intimidate as confuse him. Why would anyone wrestle a shark? And how? He'd never seen one of the notorious beasts himself, but he was fairly certain they didn't have arms. Or legs, for that matter. His mind briefly wandered, imagining what a match between a swimming pirate and a shark would look like, when he heard what sounded like . . . applause.

His captor slowed. Before them rose the ship. Someone was definitely clapping on the deck above them, and as the man released Fish, he was almost too frightened to look up. He closed his eyes for a moment, breathed in deep, and stared up toward the railing of the ship. There, leaning out over the water, with fires raging behind and all around him, stood Scab. The pirate's squat, scarred face and ringed lips twisted into a terrifying smile, and he didn't so much speak as growl, "Welcome home, Fish."